George Engelmann

Systematic Arrangement of the Species of the Genus Cuscuta

Anatiposi

George Engelmann

Systematic Arrangement of the Species of the Genus Cuscuta

Reprint of the original, first published in 1859.

1st Edition 2023 | ISBN: 978-3-38230-886-5

Anatiposi Verlag is an imprint of Outlook Verlagsgesellschaft mbH.

Verlag (Publisher): Outlook Verlag GmbH, Zeilweg 44, 60439 Frankfurt, Deutschland
Vertretungsberechtigt (Authorized to represent): E. Roepke, Zeilweg 44, 60439 Frankfurt, Deutschland
Druck (Print): Books on Demand GmbH, In de Tarpen 42, 22848 Norderstedt, Deutschland

SYSTEMATIC ARRANGEMENT

OF THE

SPECIES OF THE GENUS

CUSCUTA

WITH CRITICAL REMARKS ON OLD SPECIES AND
DESCRIPTIONS OF NEW ONES.

BY

GEORGE ENGELMANN, M.D.

*Extract from the Transactions of the Academy of Science
of St. Louis, Vol. I., No. 3, page 453.*

ST. LOUIS:
GEORGE KNAPP & CO., PRINTERS.
1859.

Systematic Arrangement of the Species of the Genus Cuscuta, *with critical Remarks on old species and Descriptions of new ones.*

By George Engelmann, M.D.

The genus Cuscuta belongs to the natural order of *Convolvulaceæ*, to which, indeed, it has been attached by almost every botanist, and from which it can not be separated, though the embryo is very distinct, being rather a minute plant than an embryo in the usual form, the tip forming a plumula, often provided with alternate scales, and without cotyledons proper. Nor ought such a natural group of plants to be split into a number of genera on subordinate characters, as has lately been proposed, and in some instances, too, upon erroneous observations.

The characters, which furnish good grounds for a subdivision of the genus, are found in the shape of the styles and stigmata and in the fruit. These same characters, it must be admitted, have been used in separating the old *Convolvuli* into numerous genera and even tribes; so that analogy would justify or even require a similar division of *Cuscuta*; but even Choisy, the author of many of these new convolvulaceous genera, in his Monograph and in De Candolle's Prodromus, admits the propriety of keeping *Cuscuta* united. Splitting *Convolvulus* into numerous genera may be excused, or perhaps justified by the necessity of separating the large crowd of species into a number of groups. This law of expediency, however, can have no scientific value, and can certainly not be pleaded in regard to such a natural, easily recognized, and not too numerous genus, as *Cuscuta* is.

The subdivisions proposed are based, as has been stated, on the shape of the styles and stigmata, and on the capsule.

The *styles*, typically always two, usually are distinct; or they are united in their whole length, or nearly so. They are of equal thickness throughout, or are thicker at base (subulate), or thickened towards the top (club-shaped); they are of equal length in one group, and unequal in another.

The *stigmata* are cylindric, elongated, and of the same thickness as the styles, or thinner; or they are oblong, or oblong-elongated, and thicker than the styles; or they are subulate from a thick base; or we find them capitate (or, as they are often, though wrongly, called, globose), hemispherical, or somewhat flattened on the upper, and flattened or usually impressed at the lower surface at the insertion of the style. In a single species, the stigmatic surface of the dilated top of the style is lobed, and in the centre somewhat depressed.

The *capsule* is either circumscissile, opening transversely by a regular joint, with thickened edges; or it bursts transversely with an irregular, jagged margin; or it remains closed (it is baccate, as it is termed), and either falls out of the persistent calyx, or it finally falls off with the calyx.

Between both styles of the ripe and dry capsule an opening is observed—the intrastylar aperture—parallel with or transverse to the dissepiment, more or less rhombic, formed by an incomplete separation of both carpels, which compose the capsule. This separation takes place in that triangular and thickest part of the dissepiment which lies next to and below the styles, and which, in the species with circumscissile fruit, adheres to the top, while the greater and thinner obcordate or bilobed part of the dissepiment remains attached to the base of the capsule in the bottom of the calyx.

In most instances the stylar portions of the dissepiment, as I will call this part, remain united at base, separating the funnel-shaped intrastylar aperture from the interior cavity of the capsule, and therefore can not give egress to the seeds, as has been erroneously stated. This is, I believe, the case with most or all American *Cuscutæ* (*Grammica*). In *Eucuscuta* and *Epistigma* the intrastylar aperture does communicate with the cells of the capsule, but the opening is far too small to let the seeds out; nor would this be necessary, as in all of them the capsule is circumscissile. In some few species I find each stylar portion of the dissepiment divided into two halves; in *C. pedicellata* these halves are widely distant from one another and adhere to the opposite halves, so as to form an opening into the capsule transverse to the dissepiment.

In *Monogynella* and *Callianche*, where the styles are united, there is, of course, no intrastylar opening, and in the former the entire dissepiment remains in the bottom of the capsule; in the latter, a small triangular stylar portion adheres to the top of the capsule, but, of course, without any opening.

Des Moulins was the first, in his "Études", to draw attention to the shape of the seed in general and the direction of the hilum in particular. Where all the four seeds are well developed, they are triangular, with a larger exterior convex and two smaller flat surfaces, the latter facing the dissepiment and the other seed of the same cell; the top of the seed is rounded or acutish; the base, with which it is attached to the placenta (which itself is dilated into a disc, often cup-shaped), is obliquely truncate or somewhat hooked, or rostrate, as Des Moulins terms it. Both flat faces of the seed are equal, or the one directed towards the dissepiment is larger than the other. At the truncate base of the seed, in the centre of a smooth and roundish umbilicus, is the hilum, forming a longer or shorter, narrower or broader linear groove, sometimes reduced almost to a point; it runs in the direction of the interior angle of the seed (*longitudinal*, DesM.), or at right angles with it (*transverse*, DesM.), or it has an intermediate, oblique direction. In some sections I find these characters sufficiently distinct; in others they seem to be less reliable; in the American *Cuscutæ* I have often found them intermediate, and variable, often in seeds from the same capsule. Wherever only one or two seeds in a capsule come to maturity their shape becomes less distinct, and offers no good characters. It is scarcely necessary to add that only ripe seeds ought to be examined; unripe ones, especially when pressed hard, have led to the strangest mistakes; winged or margined seeds, described by authors, are such unripe seeds. Nearly ripe seeds are smoother and larger, when soaked, than ripe ones.

The embryo has been supposed to offer good characters; but I have reason to believe that those embryos with one or few circumvolutions (such as the one figured by Webb, Phyt. Can. III., pl. 142, fig. 14) are taken from unripe seeds.

Another character which I at one time relied on for generic distinction of *Cuscuteæ* is found in the calyx. Usually it is gamosepalous, but in some American species it is formed of entirely distinct and imbricate sepals, not different from the surrounding bracts—a character which prevails in *Convolvulaceæ* proper, where only one genus (*Wilsonia*) is gamosepalous.

The specific characters of *Cuscutæ* are found in the thickness of the stem, but principally in the inflorescence and in the different organs of the flower and fruit.

The inflorescence together with the presence or absence of bracts within it offers good characters, less so the presence or proportion of pedicels.

The shape and proportion of calyx and corolla and of their parts (tube and lobes) furnish important but not unchangeable characters. Their texture must also be studied, and often gives an important clue to the distinction of species.

It is unnecessary to repeat what has been said by former monographers about these points, but it may not be useless to indicate a few facts not so clearly stated by them.

The tube of the calyx, generally more or less campanulate or hemispherical, is angular in some species, the angles corresponding to the commissure, or to the midrib of the sepals. Its lobes are more or less deeply divided and are often auricled at base, and overlapping; these characters, however, are not very constant and reliable, as they not rarely depend on the rich nourishment and consequent vigorous growth of the parasite. The texture of the calyx is homogeneous in some species, and either fleshy or membranaceous, (often very thin, shining, or semi-transparent, when dry,) with a small or large reticulated cellular tissue; or it exhibits, especially along the middle and towards the base an aggregation of warts or tubercles; these, also, are not constant in all the forms of the species. In other species, the tissue shows roundish or elongated pellucid dots or cells, (glands, as they are usually called,) very distinct in dried and then soaked specimens.

The tube of the corolla is cylindric or campanulate, or rather hemispherical or quite shallow, but never urceolate or ventricose during the flowering period; the swelling of the impregnated ovary, however, often gives it that shape. The laciniæ* of the corolla are of different shape, and direction, and proportion, and also sometimes auriculate and imbricate at base; their points are occasionally incurved, or their margins revolute, or involute; their margin, usually entire, is sometimes crenulate. The texture of the corolla is similar to that of the calyx, but never, I believe, verrucose, though often glandular. Its cellular structure will, yet, I suspect, offer good characters for some species, the cells being of very different size and shape in different species. The corolla, and sometimes the calyx, is occasionally covered with small papillæ, giving it a mealy appearance, which probably represent hair. This character, apparently so striking, is, however, of no more specific value than the pubescence in other plants, as I find papillose varieties of a number of European (*C. planiflora, C. Babylonica*) and American (*C. decora, etc.*) species, of course with intermediate forms. Of a single species (*C. capitata*), I know only the papillose form.

The calyx is always persistent; the corolla is deciduous only in the Indian *C. reflexa;* in all the other species it remains adhering to the capsule, either to its base, or, hood-like, to its top, or it completely envelops it, but it is not properly persistent; it is distended from the swelling of the capsule, but does not seem to grow. The position of the dead corolla is usually constant.

The stamens are mostly inserted in the very throat of the corolla, alternating with the laciniæ, but often exteriorly covered by their overlapping bases. In *Callianche* and *Monogynella* their point of insertion is usually below the throat, and the filaments very short. The filaments in the other *Cuscutæ* are more or less flattened, linear, or subulate; of different lengths, but usually much shorter than the laciniæ; they are rarely absent. The anthers are orbicular, ovate, oblong or linear, cordate or sagittate, blunt, emarginate or apic-

---

* I shall use the word *laciniæ* for the divisions of the corolla, and *lobes* for those of the calyx.

ulate, large or small; but their shape or size do not afford good and constant characters in this genus.

The most peculiar organs of the flower are the epistamineal scales, which are found in most of the species. The simplest form of that organ (in *C. inflexa, C. chlorocarpa, etc.*) exhibits a few teeth or lobes laterally adhering to the lower (attached) part of the filament. These lobes, in other species, expand into membranes, forming two lateral wings to the filament, crenulate or fringed at the tip and outside; then these wings partly unite at their upper end, thus forming a single bifid scale; finally they unite entirely, forming an oblong, ovate, spatulate or truncate, more or less crenate or fimbriate scale. Towards the base the scales are always "adnate in the middle," or, properly speaking, attached to both sides of the adnate filament. Their bases usually connect with one another, forming inverted arches.

In the following species these scales are wanting: *C. grandiflora* and *C. prismatica* of South America, *C. hyalina* of Asia, *C. Californica,* and *C. Sandwichiana.* In *C. Californica* the inverted arch alone is present, entire or fringed; in the others I find no trace of scales at all.

These scales are evidently lateral dilatations of the lower (attached) part of the filaments, perhaps of the character of stipules, as Prof. A. Braun suggests; or they are a sort of stamineal crown, attached at base to the corolla, but not a duplication of the same.

The presence, form and size of the scales furnish some of the best characters in this genus, but they are not entirely reliable; and while in some species they are very constant, in others they are found to vary considerably. It is doubtful whether a really scaleless form of *C. Europæa* exists; *C. Californica,* usually without scales, seems to occur also in a variety with scales.

The ovary and pistils are more reliable for the determination of species, just as they furnish the most important characters for the distinction of the sections. The walls of the ovary are of equal thickness throughout, or they are thickened towards the base of the style (furnished with a *stylopodium,* as I formerly designated this form.) The ovary is smaller than the tube of the corolla, or it fills its whole cavity, or even protrudes from it. The styles are subulate or terete, thick or capillary, and very constant in these differences; their length, however, is variable, and this character, so much relied on by Choisy in the subdivisions of this genus in his Monography and in DC. Prodromus, is of secondary importance, as the same species sometimes occurs with short or with long styles, and as the styles, included at first, often become exsert with age. The direction of the styles, in the flower and on the fruit, furnishes a tolerably good character.

The position of the dead corolla on the capsule has already been mentioned as a pretty reliable specific character. The shape and even the texture of the capsule also ought to be noted, though in several species (*C. Europœa*, for example) its form is quite variable.

The number of seeds which ripen in each capsule furnishes no distinction, though the species with very crowded flowers, and some others with loose flowers also, often develop only one or few seeds. The shape and surface of the seed ought to be studied more, and will, yet, it is believed, help to distinguish some species.

As almost all the characters enumerated above are subject to more or less variation, it is necessary to base the diagnosis of a species on a combination of a number of characters; but as the value of these characters is necessarily differently estimated by different botanists, some will consider as well marked species what others will look upon as mere varieties.

The different species often seem to have a predilection for certain plants, or families of plants, for their sustenance; and I have myself, at times, thought I discovered an influence of the mother plant (or, better, nursing plant, nurse) on the form and development of the parasite. But I have become fully convinced that this influence is very limited, and probably goes not even farther than the influence of different kinds of soil and manure would go with any other plant. If some species seem very constantly to prefer certain plants to others, (*C. Europœa, Urtica dioica; C. Epithymum, Calluna vulgaris,* or *Genista sagittalis; C. chlorocarpa, Polygonum; C. Gronovii, Cephalanthus; C. lupuliformis, Salix;* and, the most marked example, *C. Epilinum,* the flax fields,) it is probably because the kind of soil, the humidity or dryness, the shade or sun, and all the circumstances which suit the nurse, also agree best with the parasite. On the whole, succulent herbaceous dicotyledonous plants suit them best as nurses; some few species prefer low shrubs or semishrubs, and most of the *Monogynellæ* and a few others affect larger shrubs and trees, of course, penetrating only the tender bark of the smaller limbs.

Cuscutæ are found, also, on acrid or poisonous plants. I have seen them on *Ranunculaceæ,* on *Euphorbiæ,* on *Cicuta* and other *Umbelliferæ,* on *Rhus Toxicodendron,* and others; I have seen them, also, though sparingly and not very thrifty, on *Monocotyledoneæ,* such as *Liliaceæ, Gramineæ* and others, and even on the siliceous epidermis of *Equisetum.* The fact is, that, when once attached to a nursing stem, they throw out their branches and coil around any plant in the neighborhood, and strike their suckers into the tissue, and grow on any thing that can furnish them nourishment, even on their own branches and flowers. This is even the case with the most exclusive species, *C. Epilinum*, which attaches itself to all the weeds growing in flax fields, and may be cultivated on *Vicia*, *Impatiens*, and many other plants. Rich nourishment on succulent plants expands the organs, enlarges the flowers, increases the whole plant, and thus gives rise to varieties which at times have been distinguished as species; *C. Epithymum* in clover fields becomes what has been called *C. Trifolii ;* *C. Europæa*, on vetches, *C. Viciæ ; C. Gronovii* in shaded miry soil, on *Saururus*, *C.Saururi ;* the overgrown form of *C. Africana* is *C. Capensis, etc.*

The *haustoria* (suckers) of *Cuscuta* deeply penetrate into the tissue of the nurse, and they, with parts of the stem imbedded in this tissue, are able to reproduce the plant after all external vestiges of the stem have been rubbed off. This the gardeners often have occasion to deplore in regard to a variety of *C. Epithymum* which has become a pest to some greenhouses in Europe; I have observed the same fact in different species which I have had under cultivation, especially in *C. inflexa.*

The species of *Cuscuta* naturally arrange themselves in three large groups, distinguished by their styles and stigmata.

1. Those with *two equal styles and elongated stigmata.* They are natives of the old world, exclusively, and have rarely and only temporarily been introduced with cultivated plants into America. (*C. Epilinum* with flax into some of our Eastern States, and *C. Europæa* with vetches in Hayti.) They may be termed *Cuscuta* proper. (*Cuscuta* and *Epilinella*, Pfeiffer, Bot. Zeitg. III. 673; *Cuscuta, Epilinella*, and *Succuta*, DesM. Et. pp. 38—41.)

2. Those with *two unequal styles, and abbreviated, usually capitate, stigmata.* They abound in America and Oceanica, and in the southern and eastern parts of Asia; a few species even penetrate into western Asia and southern Europe, and a single species is found in southern Africa. Cultivation has temporarily introduced one species into Europe (*C. racemosa* from Chili, under the name of *C. suaveolens*). This group may be comprised under the name of *Grammica*, a genus established by Loureiro in his Flora Cochinchinensis, I. 212, on a species belonging here. (*Engelmannia*, Pfeiffer, Bot. Zeitg. III. 673, not Torrey & Gray, nor Klotzsch; *Pfeifferia*, Buchinger Ann. Sc. Nat. IX. 88, not Salm-Dyck; *Buchingera*, F. Schultz in Jahrb. Pharm. 1847; *Cassutha*, DesM. Et. 40 ; *Grammica*, DesM. Bull. Soc. Bot. France, I. 295.

3. Those with *styles united entirely or partly, and with capitate, ovate or conic stigmata.* The species of this group, all distinguished by their large size and thick stems, principally inhabit Asia; two extend into southern and eastern Europe, and two others are found in south Africa and southern North America. This group is Des Moulin's (Et. 39) *Monogynella*, with a little altered character.

The modifications in the form of the stigma and the dehiscence of the capsule furnish the basis for a further subdivision of the three principal groups. I will here only say, that in *Cuscuta* proper the capsule is almost always circumscissile; in *Grammica* it is often so, but more commonly it remains closed; in *Monogynella* it is constantly circumscissile.

The dead corolla covers the whole or the top of the capsule always, with a single exception (*C. Africana*), in the first; it is found on the top, or at the base of the capsule, in the second, and, if not deciduous, always on its top in the third group.

The following sections are proposed:

A. *Cuscuta Group.*

1. EUCUSCUTA. Styles nearly as long or longer and as thick or thicker than the filiform stigmata; capsule regularly circumscissile.
2. EPISTIGMA. Subulate stigmata nearly sessile; capsule opening transversely without a regular jointed separation.
3. CLISTOCOCCA. Subulate styles longer than the short subulate stigmata; capsule baccate.
4. PACHYSTIGMA. Cylindric or oblong stigmata thicker than the filiform styles; capsule bursting transversely.

B. *Grammica Group.*

5. EUGRAMMICA. Stigmata capitate; capsule more or less irregularly circumscissile.
6. CLISTOGRAMMICA. Stigmata capitate; capsule baccate.
7. LOBOSTIGMA. Top of clavate styles lobed at the upper stigmatose surface.

C. *Monogya Group.*

8. MONOGYNELLA. Stigmata capitate or ovate, united, or distinct.
9. CALLIANCHE. Stigmata conic, or almost subulate; corolla large and deciduous.

Sec. 1. *Eucuscuta.*

Styles filiform, terminating in filiform stigmata of the same length or shorter, rarely longer, and of the same thickness as the styles, or thinner towards the end. Capsule regularly circumscissile by a joint, the line of separation being thickened. Usually all four seeds ripen; they are triangular, with an obliquely truncate base, the hilum forming a narrow perpendicular line.

The flowers are mostly sessile and densely clustered, forming globose heads in the axils of single bracts without bracts in the inflorescence. The central flowers open first; the exterior ones are occasionally abortive. *C. Epithymum* has sometimes short pedicels, and *C. Babylonica* is always pedicelled. The corolla always remains on top or around the capsule, never at its base. Epistamineal scales are always present, though sometimes very thin and small, and easily overlooked.

The species of this group inhabit Europe, western and central Asia, and northern Africa to the Canary Islands.

§ 1. Styles longer than ovary.

1. C. BABYLONICA, Aucher! mss.; Choisy! Cusc. 174, t. 1, f. 1; DC. Prod.IX. 453. *C. peduncularis*, Kotschy! in sched.—Well characterized by its pedicelled flowers, truncate calyx and almost entire scales; approaching by its inflorescence to those other Asiatic species, comprised in the section *Epistigma*.—Bagdad, Aucher-Eloy! 1420 and 3183; on the Tigris, Noë! in Kurdistan, Kotschy! 388, a.

Var. ELEGANS, *C. elegans*, Boiss. & Balansa! Diag. or, II. 3, 129, from the alpine regions of the Taurus, Balansa! 708; scarcely distinct from *C. Babylonica* except by the papillose prettily rose-colored flowers, and by the scales being a little more dentate and somewhat incurved.

2. C. EPITHYMUM, Murray in Lin. syst. ed. 13. *C. Europœa*, β Lin. sp. 180. *C. minor*, Bauh, pin, 219. DC. Fl. fr. III. 644. DC. Prod. IX. 453. *C. filiformis*, β, Lam. Fl. fr. II. 307.—To this well known and common European species some authors have assigned all the different forms I am going to enumerate below, while others have separated several of them as distinct species; others, again, have united with it a number of other forms which I must consider distinct, especially such as I class with *C. planiflora;* some have even mixed up with it the very distinct *C. Europœa*.

It is certainly difficult to make precise the limits of *C. Epithymum* and *C. planiflora*, and some forms which I class under var. *Kotschyi* of the former, and others which fall under var. *approximata* of the latter, apparently are more closely allied than the extremes of either species among themselves; while the common *C. Epithymum*, especially the form known as *C. Trifolii*, is as distinct as can be from Tenore's original *C. planiflora*. I arrange the different forms in the following order:

Var. α. VULGARIS, the common form of central Europe extending west to Great Britain, north to Scandinavia, south to northern Spain (Bourgeau! 655), northern Italy (*C. acutiflora*,

Rota! and also Naples, to the Crimea, and reaching east-wardly far into Asia (Caucasus, Hohenacker! 409 and 1939, Altai, Ledebour! "Orient" Herb. Tournefort!) It varies considerably, especially in the size and proportion of the calyx and its lobes, and transition forms, uniting it with the other varieties, are not rare. I have paid some attention to the proportion of the stigma and style, but find no perma-nent character in them; the style proper is longer or shorter than the stigmatic portion; and this part is cylindrical or subulate in specimens not otherwise distinguishable; the stig-ma is usually pale brown-red, or, when dry, dark red, rarely yellowish.—*C. Trifolii*, Babington! sometimes so fatal to whole clover fields in England, France, Switzerland, Germany, and Sweden, is a luxuriant form, overgrown at the expense of the succulent herb, which it destroys.

Var. β. MACRANTHERA; *C. macranthera*, Heldr. & Sart.! in sched.; Boiss.! diag. or, II. 3, 126; *C. Calliopes*, Heldr. & Sart.! Boiss.! ibid, 128.—Large flowers on very short pedicels; calyx short, its ovate lobes scarcely covering half of the tube of the corolla; laciniæ ovate, acute or obtusish; anthers oval, large, often longer than the filaments; scales usually shorter than the tube, sometimes quite narrow.—A southern form, found on the southern declivity of the Alps, in Piedmont, Tyrol, Spain (Willkomm! 52, a), in southern France, in It-aly (on the Apennines and in Corsica), in Greece and in the Crimea; I have also seen, in the Kew Herbarium, an Eng-lish specimen of this variety, on *Ulex;* it has made its appearance in green-houses on *Erica* and other evergreen shrubs; this garden form is *C. xanthonema* of the Paris Jar-din des Plantes.

Var. γ.? OBTUSATA; this very curious form was collected by Funk! (Herb. Cosson and Hb. Reichenbach) in the Sierra Nevada of Spain on some shrubby *Genista;* the glomerules consist of 3-5 flowers, only, on pedicels longer than the calyx; lobes of calyx and corolla broadly oval, obtuse, shorter than the tube of the corolla; scales large; styles as in the com-mon form. I would, at once, have acknowledged this pecu-liar plant as a distinct species, if a second specimen had not come to hand, collected by Heldreich on *Artemisia* near Ko-niah in the interior of Asia Minor, which approaches more to the ordinary form; flowers similar, but smaller, sessile, 6-8 in a small head; scales narrow; styles ordinary, seeds very small (0.3 lines diam.) The former may be distinguished as var. *macropoda*, the latter as var. *apoda*.

Var. δ.? SAGITTANTHERA*; allied to var. *angustiloba*, distin-

---

* Philologists will blame this "vox hybrida," but daily experience teaches us and philological research confirms, that words are not formed

guished by the loose glomerules; pedicels as long as calyx; lobes of calyx obtusish, scarcely as long as tube of corolla; laciniæ lanceolate, acute; anthers broadly sagittate; scales large, crenulate; styles subulate at base, on the capsule almost horizontally divaricate.—Tunis, Kralik! in Herb. Cosson and Herb. Mus. Florent.—the only African form of the group of *Epithymum* seen.

Var. *ε.* ANGUSTATA; I distinguish by this name an Italian which assumes different shapes, described under different form, names. It has narrow and elongated lobes of the corolla and usually also of the calyx, which is commonly longer than the tube of the corolla; the flowers are numerous and sessile, or ordinarily more or less pedicelled. Three varieties may be distinguished.

Var. a. *alba*, with whitish stems, smaller flowers, membranaceous calyx. This is the true *C. alba*, Presl! Del. Prag. 87, also of Tenore and some other Italian botanists, while most authors apply this name to the original *C. planiflora*, Ten. Presl's description, copied by almost every subsequent author, is very erroneous; but his own specimens, on *Zizyphus*, preserved in his collection at Prague, and in the imperial Herbarium at Vienna, leave no doubt about the identity of the plant. *C. subulata*, Tineo! in Gussone Fl. Sic. II. 888, is exactly the same thing, as also *C. Gussoni*, Gasparrini! in Hb. It is a southern form occurring principally in Sicily, also about Naples and in Malta; it is often found on shrubs, and Sieber! (in Herb. Ledebour) gathered it on an oak.

Var. b. *angustissima*, flowers longer than in any other form seen (2¼—2½ lines long), on short pedicels, with short calyx, slender elongated tube, narrowly lanceolate acuminate laciniæ, distinctly subulate filaments, and rather small scales. In fields of Medicago near Padua, Visiani!

Var. c. *rubella*, with red stems, larger flowers, red calyx of a thicker texture. This is *C. planiflora*, Koch fl. Germ., DesM. Et. 54, and many other authors, but not of Tenore. It has often been collected in southern Tyrol on *Colutea*, *Artemisia*, etc.; it also occurs in the Abruzzi and in Corsica.

Var. *ζ.* KOTSCHYI; *C. Kotschyi*, Des Moulins! Études p. 56, (not *C. Kotschyana* Boiss); *C. microcephala*, Welwitsch! in sched. Flor. Lusitan. nro. 1048.—This plant is perhaps the original *Epithymum* of the old botanists, as it often occurs on *Thymus* and other small frutescent *Labiatæ*. It is well characterized by rather thick red stems, the

according to theories, nor languages in the closet. The actual necessities of a living people are not bound by such rules of unity, as little as these prevail in the formation of nations, the present fashionable theory of political nationalities to the contrary notwithstanding.

small and dense glomerules, the closely sessile flowers, with long acute or acuminate lobes of calyx and corolla, and rather shorter styles than the common form of *C. Epithymum*. When the base of the calyx is elongated into a pedicel, it becomes the form just mentioned as *rubella*.—On the higher mountains of southern Europe, the southern declivity of the Alps, the mountains of the Dauphinée, the Pyrenees, the Sierra Nevada and other mountain regions of Spain and Portugal; in the Abruzzi of southern Italy, in the mountains of central Sicily, of Turkey, and of Greece.

Var. *scabrella* from Sicily, Gussone! and Arragon, Webb! is a papillose form of the same plant.

3. C. ABYSSINICA, Richard, Abyss. II. 78. *C. macrostyla*, Decaisne in Herb. Mus. Paris., seems to be well distinguished by the short and thick lobes of the calyx, the very long and narrow, erect laciniæ, the small, often bifid, scales and the very long capillary styles. These even surpass those of the last species, while the other characters, together with the crowded, closely sessile flowers, approach it to the next one. The typical form was collected on *Lantana;* another, with shorter laciniæ, was gathered on a leguminous shrub.

4. C. PLANIFLORA, Tenore, sensu latiori. This name has, like that of *C. alba*, suffered under the misfortune scarcely ever to be applied to the species, on which the author originally bestowed it! The difficulty was increased by an incomplete description and by Prof. Tenore himself inadvertently distributing under his new name a form of *C. Epithymum;* even now he preserves in his own herbarium, under this name, forms of several other species, besides the very specimen, described and figured by him as *C. planiflora*, easily recognized by the well figured *Plantago lanceolata* on which it grows. But this is not the only, nor the principal, cause of the difficulties under which botanists have labored in regard to this plant. It is probably the most variable of all the species of this genus, and appears under a larger number of forms than any other. Well may botanists differ from the view that I take in regard to this species, but it has not been adopted lightly. With 150 to 200 specimens from Europe, Africa, and Asia, before me, I have found it impossible to separate, specifically, the different forms here brought together; and even the subspecies, enumerated below, can not always be limited satisfactorily. On the other hand I find it difficult to keep this species, or complex of forms, as I am inclined to call it, separate from some allied species. Some varieties approach to *C. brevistyla* others to *C. Palæstina*, and others again are difficult to distinguish from the alpine form of *C. Epithymum (Kotschyi)*.

The long list of synonyms properly belongs to the different subspecies; for the species, as I take it, no synonym, nor even a name, exists: the one adopted by me is the earliest one given to any one of the forms.

Synopsis of the forms of C. planiflora.

a. Lobes of the calyx more membranaceous than fleshy; laciniæ of the corolla turgid only at the points; styles much longer than ovary.

> * Calyx cupulate, lobes usually broad and short, and, like the short laciniæ, cuspidate: Var. *approximata.*
> ** Calyx more deeply divided, its lobes and the laciniæ narrow, elongated, acute: Var. *Schiraziana.*

b. Lobes of the calyx thick and turgid; laciniæ turgid and often cucullate at tip; styles longer than ovary, usually shorter or as long as capsule.

> * Flowers larger; lobes of calyx united above the middle or almost to the point: Var. *Webbii.*
> ** Flowers usually smaller; sepals almost distinct.
> † Flowers smooth: Var. *Tenorii.*
> †† Flowers mealy or warty: Var. *papillosa.*

Var. *a.* APPROXIMATA; *C. approximata*, Babington! Ann. & Mag. Nat. Hist., 1844, pl. 4., and 1845 pl. 1.; A. Braun! Berl. bot. Zeitg., 1844, p. 542, and in Jahrb. d. Ver. f. N. K. Nassau, 1851, t. 1, f. 1; *C. urceolata*, Kunze! in Flora, 1846, p. 651; *C. cupulata*, Engelm.! in Bot. Zeitg., 1846, p. 276; *C. planiflora*, Kunze! in Flora, 1846, p. 655; *C. leucosphœra*, Boiss. & Heldr.! in sched. (afterwards referred by Boissier diag. or 1. II. 127 to *C. urceolata); C. Asiatica*, Pallas! in Herb. H. Bot. Petropol.—The name, *approximata*, was given to this species for the closely approaching halves of the scales; yet, it more appropriately signifies the close alliance with the last species, and especially with its last mentioned variety. The original *C. approximata* was found in fields of *Medicago* in England, Germany and Switzerland, undoubtedly an imported plant, as Babington already states, probably from India; or perhaps from southeastern Europe or Asia Minor. In this cultivated plant the flowers are larger ($1\frac{3}{4}$—2 lines long) more attenuated at base, the scales appressed, short and often bifid. Similar forms, with numerous large flowers in large and very dense heads occur in Asia Minor, (Taurus, Kotschy! 357; Tmolus, Balansa! 414; Smyrna, Balansa! 412; Bithynia, Thirke!) in Greece (Taygetus! Parnassus! Thracia!) and in Piedmont (Herb. Link! Reichenbach fil.! The plants from the southwest seem to be a little smaller; Spain (Willkomm! 263 & 246; Bourgeau! 331, & 1299; Ph. Schimper!) Several specimens from the Canary Islands belong rather to this than to *C. Episonchum.* In the east this species has been found in Egypt (Fischer!) in Syria (Kotschy! 104) in Persia (Kotschy! 580, a.) and in the Himalaya regions (Hügel! Stocks! Hooker & Thomson!) The northern Asiatic form, which I had formerly distinguished under the name of *C. cupulata*, occurs in the Caucasus, the Altai, and, as it seems, throughout Siberia, (Ledebour! Godet! Becker! Karelin! 1721, etc.); flowers smaller in dense but small heads; calyx large, loose, almost entire, with broad and short lobes; scales comparatively large and incurved.

Var. β. SCHIRAZIANA; *C. Schiraziana*, Boissier! diag. or. I. 9, 86, has loose and few flowered heads, rather membranaceous flowers with the lobes of the deeply divided calyx and the laciniæ long and acute. The specimens examined by me, the same that Boissier described, were collected in Persia by Kotschy! and distributed under 118 and 318. In some the laciniæ are larger, in others shorter; scales larger and entire; or smaller, truncate and even bifid.—Link gathered a specimen of this form in Portugal on *Ulex nanus*, which has even longer lobes and a more deeply divided calyx than the Persian plant.

Var. γ. WEBBII; *C. Episonchum*, Webb! Phyt. Canar. III. p. 36, t. 141; *C. Epiplocamum*, Webb! in Pl. Bourgeau, 1430. —This, together with *C. calycina*, Webb, another form of this species, seems to be the only native *Cuscuta* of the Canary Islands, though the Herbaria show the names of *C. Europæa* and *C. Epithymum* from thence; *C. Epilinum* has been introduced there. It has been collected by Webb! Bourgeau! 18, 426, 459, 1430; De la Perraudière! Bolle! and others. I have seen the same form from Portugal, Deakin! Welwitsch! 192.—In *C. Episonchum* the lobes of the calyx are not as completely united as in *C. Epiplocamum*.

Var. δ. TENORII; *C. planiflora*, Tenore! Syll. Fl. Neap. p. 128 and Flor. Neap. III. p. 250, t. 220, f. 3.—If I am not mistaken, Kunze (Flora, 1846, p. 655, in plant Willk. nro. 303) was the only botanist who recognized Tenore's plant; every other author has bestowed the name on some other forms of our plant or on some other species. *C. planiflora*, Koch! Germ. p. 570, and Reichenb. Fl. Germ. exsicc. nro. 2069, are forms of *C. Epithymum*.—Tenore's plant is most common in Sicily and north Africa, extending to the Canary Islands, to Spain, southern France, Italy and the Mediterranean islands, to Greece and Egypt, and undoubtedly also to Asia Minor and Syria. It is one of the smallest *Cuscutæ*, the heads are compact, 2—3 lines in diameter, white or rose-colored. The turgidity of the almost cylindric lobes of the calyx and of the laciniæ is very distinct even in the dried specimen, and very striking in the fresh or soaked one. Flowers often less than 1 line in length; grains very rough, 0.3—0.4 lines in diameter.—This is *C. alba* of most authors, but not of Presl; *Succuta*, DesM. Et. 41 is a genus founded on an immature specimen of the same plant; *C. Epithymum*, Gussone! Flor.

Inarim. p. 212, Cosson! in Plant. Bourgeau and of many authors on plants of southern Europe; *C. Europœa*, Bové! in Hb. Mauritan, 149; *C. bracteosa*, Gaspar.! in Hb.; *C. microcephala*, d'Escayrac! in Hb; *C. Godronii*, DesM.! l. c. 60, is a form with more acute lobes of calyx and corolla. *C. Sicula*, Tineo (fide spec. in the Hb. Cesati) is the same plant with lobes of the calyx a little broader; *c. calycina*, Webb! Phyt. Canar. III. p. 37, t. 152, has a larger calyx including almost entirely the corolla; *C. Canariensis*, Choisy! Mss. is the same thing.—It occurs in many published collections; besides those already mentioned it has been distributed by Bourgeau! 491, 1298, 1430,a. etc.; Aucher–Eloy! 1418; Huet de Pavillon! Palermo, etc.

Var. *ε*. PAPILLOSA is a peculiar form of the last subspecies, which thus far seems to have escaped observers; the whole flower is covered with semi-transparent papillæ; otherwise, I find no difference in specimens sent from Algiers to the Paris Museum by Balansa! But often the lobes are elongated and acute; so in the specimens from Tunis, Kralik! 410, Algiers, Cosson! Segovia, Hb. Gussone! A specimen from Arabia, Botta! in Hb. Mus. Paris, seems also to belong here. *C. globulosa*, Boiss. & Reut. is very closely allied to this form, and distinguished principally by the very short styles, and the globose corolla, the lobes of which cover the capsule; this form of the corolla does, however, occasionally also occur in specimens, which can not be separated from *C. planiflora*.

5. C. PALÆSTINA, Bossier! diag. or. I. 11, 86.—This pretty little species is closely allied to the last, to which the author himself subsequently referred it; but it seems to hold its rank with a number of other species of this genus, the limits of which are so difficult to ascertain. Tournefort (Cor. 45) already distinguished it under the name of *C. Cretica;* it is also *C. micrantha*, Tineo! in Gussone Fl. Sic. Syn. II. 887, not Choisy; and *C. capillaris*, Reichenb. Pl. Crit. V. 64. —It grows on small mostly shrubby plants, on arid hills in the Mediterranean region; in Sicily, Tineo! Morea, Bory! Attica, Heldreich! Creta, Sieber! Raulin! and other Grecian islands, Lefèvre! etc.; Palestine, Boissier! Gaillardot! Blanche!—Heads only about 2 lines in diameter, flowers ½–1 line long, usually 4, but often only 3-parted; only the central or primitive flower of the heads is often 5-parted; calyx comparatively large, with broad and short carinate lobes; top of laciniæ cucullate; scales rather large, broadly spatulate, incurved; styles somewhat longer than ovary.

§ 2. Styles as long or shorter than ovary.

6. C. BREVISTYLA, A. Braun! in Pl. Schimp, and in Rich-

ard Tent. Fl. Abyss. II. 79, is perhaps too nearly allied to
C. planiflora, from some forms of which it is scarcely distinguished but by the short styles, which, in fruit, become divaricate. In the original Abyssinian specimens the lobes of
the corolla are expanded, in some others they are closed over
the capsule. The scales are short, thin and truncate or sometimes bilobed.—It has been found in Abyssinia, Schimper!
III. 1486; on the Sinai, Botta! in Persia, Kotschy! 580;
Affghanistan, Griffith! 686; Thibet, Hooker and Thomson!
C. elegans, Noë! in Herb. 518 (not Boissier), from the Tigris,
is the same plant.

Var. ? GLOBULOSA; *C. globulosa*, Boissier & Reuter! in
sched., Boiss. in Diag. or. II. 3, 126; *C. Balansæ*, Boiss. &
Reut. in sched.—This very pretty form at first sight looks
very distinct; but Boissier himself already suggests the propriety of uniting it with " *C. alba*" (*planiflora*), and indeed
its papillose flowers greatly resemble the var. *papillosa* described above; on the other hand it approaches *C. capitata*,
but more in external appearance than in essential characters;
the pretty red tinge of its flowers is occasionally found in
both of these, and may be in some connection with the development of the papillæ.—The corolla closes over the capsule, giving the flower as well as the whole head an obtuse appearance; the scales in the original specimen are bilobed,
in the other truncate; styles very short.—Mountain regions
of Asia Minor: on the Tmolus, Balansa! 413; on the Taurus,
the same! 707.

7. C. EUROPÆA, Lin. sp. 180, excl. var. β. This well known
and well characterized species offers none of the difficulties
of all the other European *Cuscutæ ;* the obconic calyx with
its thick and fleshy and usually elongated base and thin and
obtuse lobes, the thin corolla with obtuse laciniæ, the small
and very thin bifid or truncate appressed scales, the large
ovary and comparatively large capsule with short divaricate
styles and bearing the dead corolla only on top (not enveloped in it) readily distinguish it; nor does it vary near as
much as the others do; the flowers, however, are as often 5
as 4-parted.

This species has given cause to a good deal of discussion
in regard to the presence or absence of scales; but though I
have examined a number of specimens said to have no scales,
among others the original Var. *nefrens* of Sweden, I have
never failed to discover that organ, though sometimes in a
very defective state; I, therefore, can not doubt that it is always present, but frequently so small and especially so very
thin as to escape detection. In dry specimens, soaked or boil-
ed, it adheres to the tube of the corolla so closely, that it is
scarcely possible to see or to separate it; but it is readily dis-

covered and detached in the dry flower, if not too much mashed in pressing. The scales are rarely rounded, oftener truncate, and toothed at the apex, most commonly bifid, and fimbriate or toothed, or consisting of two distinct lateral dentate or entire, often extremely small, lobes.

The capsule is commonly depressed, but a form with an elevated, conic capsule, var. *conocarpa*, is not rare; both often grow together and can not be distinguished otherwise.

Var. *Indica* has more crowded, smaller flowers, and perhaps a little longer styles. A specimen from Sarepta on *Alhagi Camelorum*, in the Herbarium of the St. Petersburg Bot. Garden, has still smaller flowers, but shows no other, to me, appreciable difference.

Var. *Viciæ* has often a more solid texture of the flower and fruit, which last does not open before full maturity, and may thus in herbaria sometimes seem to be indehiscent, while, usually, the capsules of dried specimens readily open long before they are quite ripe. A specimen from Hayti has larger flowers, fruit and seed, than any other I have seen.

C. Europæa inhabits the greater part of Europe and the mountains of Asia to the Himalaya. I have seen no specimens from Africa, or from Spain south of the Pyrenees, from Sicily or Greece; in Italy it grows near Rome! and Naples! also in Asia Minor! on the Caucasus! in Persia! Affghanistan! Thibet! and on the Himalaya! in general. Once, only, it seems to have been seen in America; Poiteau! in Herb. Neufchatel, gathered it on *Vicia* in Hayti, where it no doubt was introduced from Europe.

The following formidable list of synonyms shows how much this species has exercised botanists.

C. major, Bauh. Pin. 219, DC. Fl. fr. III. 644; DC.! Prodr. IX. 452; *C. filiformis*, *a*, Lam. Fl. fr. II. 307; *C. tetrandra*, Mœnch Meth. 461; *C. vulgaris*, Pers. Syn. I. 289; *C. tubulosa*, Presl! Del. 215; *C. Epithymum*, Thuil. Fl. Par. 85, not Lin.; *C. Epicnidea*, Bernhardi Thur. Gartz. 1844, nro. 4; *C. halophyta*, Fries! n. mant. I. 8; *C. halophila!* Sum. Veg. I. 191; *C. monogyna*, Schmidt, Fl. Bohem. and in some herbaria, not Vahl.; *C. Ligustri*, Areschoug, Revis. Cusc. Suec. p. 17; *C. tetrasperma*, Jan! in sched.; *C. hyalina*, Boiss.! in sched., not Roth. *C. Segetum*, Rota in Giorn. bot. ital. II. 247, and *C. Viciæ*, Schultz, ap. DesM. are overgrown and often very destructive forms on fields of *Vicia*, *Medicago*, etc.—*C. Epitriphyllum*, Bernh.l. c. 1844, nro. 4; *C. Schkuhriana*, Pfeiff. Bot. Zeit., 1845, p. 673. *C. Europæa*, var. *nefrens* Fries! Sum. Veg. I. 191, and var. *vacua* Gren. & God., Fl. fr. II. 504, are names given to a supposed form without scales.—Var. *Pontica*, C. Koch in Linnæa XIX. 19, I have not seen. *C. brachystyla*, C. Koch! in Lin. XXII.

747, is a form with often patulous laciniæ and with conic capsule. *C. capillaris*, Edgeworth! Lin. Transact. XX. 68, is a more densely glomerate form from the Himalaya, with short laciniæ and very short bifid scales.

8. C. KURDICA, n. sp.: caulibus capillaceis; glomerulis parvis paucifloris bractea ovata acuminata suffultis; floribus arcte sessilibus plerumque 4-meris; calycis fere ad basin divisi lobis ovato-lanceolatis acutis crassiusculis tubum corollæ superantibus; laciniis ovato-lanceolatis erectis seu conniventibus (demum capsulæ arcte cinctæ adpressis) tubo fere longioribus; staminibus quam laciniæ multo brevioribus, antheris parvis subrotundis apiculatis filamento vix brevioribus; squamis basi tubi affixis parvis hyalinis tenuissimis truncatis; stylis ovario paulo, capsula depressa multo brevioribus.

On the Gara mountain, Kurdistan, Kotschy! Pl. Al. Kurd. 388, b. under the name of *C. minor*, fide Choisy and *C. alpina*, Hohenacker, in sched.; Kurdistan, J. Brant! in Hb. Hooker.—In texture and habit resembling *C. Europæa*, but scales even yet thinner; flowers fewer, more closely sessile; lobes of calyx and corolla acute; corolla on the fruit globose, closely investing the whole capsule; styles very short and slender, not as much divaricate as in the allied species.— Flowers 1 line long; seeds large in proportion, 0.5–0.6 lines long.

9. C. PERSICA, DeCaisne in Hb. Mus. Par.: caule filiformi; floribus sessilibus arcte glomeratis bractea ovata seu orbiculata suffultis; calycis campanulati lobis ovatis acutis corollæ tubum superantibus; laciniis tubo vix longioribus ovatis abrupte acuminatis sæpe papillosis, erectis demum patulis; staminibus brevibus; squamis spatulatis laciniato-fimbriatis faucem acquantibus incurvis; stylis brevibus subulatis vix ad medium stigmatosis in capsula tenuíssima depressa corolla investita suberectis.

Ispahan, Persia, Aucher-Eloy! Herbier d'Orient in Hb. Mus. Paris, without number, apparently on some species of *Lactuca.*—A very distinct species, of which a single specimen only has come under my observation. The tough corolla totally invests and, as it would seem, supports the extremely thin capsule, just as in *C. capitata*, to which it is also allied by the subulate styles; scales larger than in any allied form, their fringes covering the top of the capsule.— Flowers 1½ lines long, seeds ½ line long, strongly reticulate.

10. C. EPILINUM, Weihe, Archiv. d. Apoth. VIII. 54, (1824); DC. Prod. IX. 452; *C. densiflora*, Soyer-Willem. An. Soc. Lin. Paris I. 26 (1822) only by name; description l. c. IV. 281 (1826); *C. major*, Koch & Ziz, Cat. pal. 5; *C. vulgaris*, Presl, cech. 56; *Epilinella cuscutoides*, Pfeiff. Bot. Zeit. Oct. 1845, p. 673; DesM. Et. 64.—This well known and

very distinct species of the flax fields of Europe, (Russia! Sweden! Germany! France! England! Ireland! Spain! Sicily!) extends into the Canary Islands (Webb! Finlay!) and Egypt (Kralik! Figari!) and has also been seen in the eastern parts of the United States! I have seen no specimens from Asia, but Roxburgh's *C. aggregata*, Fl. Ind. I. 447, "introduced into the botanic garden of Calcutta with flax from Bagdad," is most probably the same thing.

The characters relied on for a generic separation of this species from *Cuscuta*, are untenable, or are founded on mistake. The calyx is deeply 5-lobed, not 5-sepaled; the capsule is constructed exactly as in the allied species; the dissepiment is complete till, at maturity, the larger, lower, obcordate part separates from the upper substylar portion. The intrastylar aperture penetrates into the capsule only at full maturity by a slit parallel to the dissepiment and sometimes by a second transverse one. The stigma is, at the flowering period, almost twice as long as the style, and at base of the same thickness, slightly tapering to an obtuse point; only in fruit, when the style is shrivelled, the stigma has the appearance of being club-shaped.

The very short style, the shape of the thick stigma and the structure of the stylar part of the dissepiment, indicate a close alliance to the Asiatic species, enumerated below, though all these have pedicelled, and not, like our species, closely sessile flowers. It is not improbable that it originally came from Asia or from Egypt.

Sec. 2. *Epistigma.*

Styles none or consisting of a very short knob on each half of the ovary; stigmata cylindric or subulate, usually of the length of the ovary. The capsule separates from the base only at complete maturity in a ragged line, not by a regular joint; the opening is wide (*C. pedicellata*) or very small (*C. Arabica, C. pulchella*); the emarginate dissepiment remains in the base of the capsule, as in *Eucuscuta*; the withered corolla closely coats the capsule.

The distinctly pedicelled flowers are disposed in loose or compact umbelliform clusters, few-flowered or crowded, supported by a single bract.

The species belonging here are all Asiatic; *C. Arabica* extends into Egypt, where it seems to be the most common form.

This group constitutes the connecting link between *Eucuscuta* and *Callianche*, another Asiatic form, in which the little remnants of the styles are united.

11. C. Kotschyana, Boiss. Diag. or, I. 7, 29 (not *C. Kotschyi*, DesM.); well characterized by the large (2 lines long)

flowers with a large, loose, cup-shaped calyx and acuminate
laciniæ; fruit unknown.—Southern Persia, Kotschy! 749.   I
refer here a specimen from the Herbarium of the St. Petersburg botanic garden, collected in Armenia by Szovits, though
the flowers are a little smaller and the calyx is rather more
deeply divided.

12. C. PULCHELLA, n. sp.: umbellis laxis paucifloris bractea ovata acuminata suffultis; calycis carnosi lobis ovatis acutis corollæ tubum subæquantibus; laciniis tubo fere æquilongis ovatis acutis papillosis crenulatis erectis seu patulis;
staminibus brevioribus, antheris ovatis filamenta subulata
æquantibus; squamis angustis faucem attingentibus fimbriatis incurvis; stigmatibus ovarium globoso-ovatum apice sub-
conicum æquantibus; capsula corolla connivente tota involuta apertura parva basilari demum dehiscente.

Var. β. ALTAICA, calyce profundius fisso; laciniis acutiori-
bus; squamis minoribus sæpe bifidis.

Affghanistan, Griffith! 688–691, in Hb. Hooker, on *Al-*
hagi, Peganum, Artemisia, etc. β. Sarepta! originally from
the Hb. of Pallas, and Altai, Sievers! both in the Herbarium of the Botanic Garden of St. Petersburg; Griffith's
plant, which may be distinguished as a. *Affghana,* has beau-
tifully bright red stems and flowers; the very fleshy calyx
especially is bright colored; umbels 4–6-flowered, pedicels
as long as calyx or as the whole flower; flower 1½ lines long;
capsule opening late and with a very small circular aperture.
—From *C. Kotschyana* it is distinguished by the much smaller flowers with longer pedicels, the deeply divided calyx, the
ovate and not acuminate laciniæ.—The Altaic specimens may
possibly constitute *C. Asiatica,* Pallas, but the specimen in
Hb. H. B. Petropol., labeled thus by himself, belongs to *C.*
planiflora, var. *approximata.*

13. C. PEDICELLATA, Ledeb.! Fl. Altaic. I. 293. Icon. t.
234. DC. Prod. IX. 453, excl. syn.—The smallest flowered
species of this section; flowers scarcely one line long, whitish,
of very thin texture; scales small, truncate; styles almost united at base, separating in the ripe fruit; intrastylar aperture
transverse to the dissepiment; top of thin capsule separating from the base with a very large opening, rather irregularly torn; more closely allied to the next than to both other
species of this section; distinguished from it principally by
the much smaller flowers and the wide opening of the ripe
capsule. I have seen no other specimens but Ledebour's own,
collected on the Altai, parasitic on some species of *Galium;*
the other specimens referred to this species by authors do
not belong here.

14. C. ARABICA, Fresenius! Pl. Ægypt. p. 165; Choisy!
Cusc. 175, t. 1, f. 2, and DC. Prod. IX. 453; not of Wight;

Cassuta Arabica, DesM. Et. 72.—A well marked species, the most common one in Egypt and extending to the eastern shore of the Red Sea. It was collected in the former country by Bové! 354; Aucher-Eloy! 1418; S. Fischer! Kralik! and before all these by Lippi! in Hb. Vaillant, where it is labeled as " Cuscuta sulphurei coloris Ægyptiaca, flore niveo," etc. Arabia, on the Sinai, Rueppell! Schimper! nro. 140.—I can not see how it is possible to ascribe to it capitate stigmata, nor is the capsule exactly baccate; this last error, however, is easily accounted for, as only the fully ripe capsule will separate from the base, and with quite a small opening.— The Sinai plant, the original *C. Arabica*, has shorter pedicels, denser glomerules, cordate-sagittate anthers, and larger, even incurved, scales. Var. *Ægyptiaca* is distinguished by its longer pedicels, looser umbel, rather orbicular anthers, and smaller, often bifid, scales, which sometimes seem to be reduced to mere teeth; it may possibly be the luxuriant form, corresponding to *C. Trifolii* and growing on cultivated plants.

Sec. 3. *Clistococca.*

This group, represented by a single Asiatic species, is closely allied to *Epistigma*, but distinguished from it and all its other allies by the really baccate capsule, which at maturity separates from the persistent calyx, entirely covered by the closely enveloping corolla. The styles are subulate, much thicker at base, usually longer than the thin and pointed stigma. Flowers sessile, densely clustered.

15. C. CAPITATA, Roxb. Fl. Ind. I. 448; *C. rosea*, Jacquemont! in Hb.—Roxburgh's description, as far as it goes, agrees well enough with the species I take for it, which is, so far as I know, the only papillate Cuscuta in India; but it seems to be far from common there; it is, on the contrary, confined to the mountain districts and to an elevation of from 6 to 12,000 feet.—The lanceolate lobes of the deeply slit calyx and corolla are covered with hemispherical or subcylindric papillæ, consisting of numerous very minute cells. Scales in the lower part of the tube, not reaching to the middle, rounded or bilobed, dentate. Styles as long as ovary, much shorter than capsule. Capsule very thin and fragile, but strengthened by the dry corolla forming a tough coating over it; intrastylar aperture large.—Flowers over 1½ lines long, often rose-colored; seed oval, 0.6 lines long.

India "in great abundance on *Crotalaria juncea*," Roxburgh; on the Himalaya, on some *Artemisia*, Jacquemont! 1550; on *Thymus*, 7—10,000 feet high, Thomson! in Kumaun, 12,000 feet high, Strachney & Winterbottom! nro.

3, in part (in some herbaria the Indian form of *C. Euro-paea* is preserved under this number).

Sec. 4. *Pachystigma.*

Stigmata cylindric or oblong, obtuse, thicker than the fili-form styles. Capsules bursting transversely, late, and not by a proper joint. Seeds compressed, indistinctly triangular, obliquely truncate at base, with a very short perpendicular or slightly oblique hilum.

Flowers pedicelled, disposed in a loose fascicled inflores-cence; pedicels usually supported by bracts, only the latest ones naked. Corolla remaining on the top, or, in *C. Africana*, at the base of the capsule.

The three species of this group inhabit Southern Africa, and are usually parasitic on evergreen shrubs. The form of the stigma is intermediate between that of *Eucuscuta* and of *Grammica*, and the inflorescence is similar to that of the latter.

16. C. ANGULATA, n. sp.; caulibus filiformibus; bracteis lineari-lanceolatis; pedicellis capillaceis flore longioribus (ul-timis brevioribus) ramosis laxe fasciculatis; calycis profunde 5-partiti ad commissuras alato-angulati lobis late ovatis ob-tusis tubum corollæ late campanulatum superantibus; la-ciniis corollæ ovatis obtusis demum patulis stamina æquanti-bus; antheris obtusis basi profunde cordatis filamento subu-lato vix brevioribus; squamis ovatis fimbriatis tubum fere excedentibus incurvis; pistillis ovario parvo depresso-globoso bis terve longioribus tubum excedentibus, stigmatibus cylin-dricis seu subclavatis stylo ipso brevioribus.— *C. Africana*, Choisy! Cusc. 176 and DC. Prod. IX. 454, pro parte, fide spec. in Hb. De Cand. et cit. nec descript; *C. Africana, c.* Drege! in sched.

Cape of Good Hope, Dutuitskloof, 3000 feet high, on *Staavia*, Drege! Mund & Maire! Harvey! in Hb. Hook-er; Roxburgh! in Hb. Lambert, now Delessert.—The broad and short flowers with broadly oval and obtuse lobes and the 5-angled, or rather winged calyx, distinguish this spe-cies at first sight from both its allies. Choisy has con-founded it with his *C. Africana*, as not only his reference to Drege's specimen but also his own label to this same speci-men in DeCandolle's authentic herbarium prove.—Flowers about 1¼–1½ lines long, 1¾ wide when fully expanded; styles usually longer than stigmata, only in very young flowers of the same length. Fruit and seed not seen.

17. C. NITIDA, E. Meyer! in sched.; Choisy! Cusc. 177, t. 2, f. 1 and DC. Prod. IX. 454.—Well distinguished by the broad and acute lobes of the calyx, the narrowly lanceolate acute laciniæ and the stigmata which usually are much longer than

the styles, rarely of the same length. Stamens half as long as laciniæ; incurved scales as long or sometimes longer than tube; capsule irregularly circumscissile.

This is *C. Africana, a.* Drege! *C. Africana,* Ecklon & Zeyher! 20, 77, 11, and 21, 1, 11; *C. Burmanni,* Choisy! Cusc. 177, & DC. Prod. IX. 454, is the same plant, as I have satisfied myself by a careful examination of the original specimen in Hb. Delessert. This specimen is further interesting as it bears the inscription *"C. Americana,"* it would seem, in Thunberg's handwriting. This may therefore be the original plant, which Thunberg first took for Linnæus' *C. Americana* and afterwards named *C. Africana,* so that *C. nitida* would be the true Thunbergian *Africana ;* but even if this be so, it will be better to leave the nomenclature as at present established, especially as quite probably Thunberg confounded both species. Another fact, bearing on this question, is, that in Jussieu's Herb., now in the Museum of the Jardin des Plantes, a specimen of *C. Chinensis* is preserved, labeled " *C. Americana, Thunb. C. B. Sp. Thunberg ded.*" So it seems that at one time Thunberg himself took *C. Chinensis* for his *Americana,* but as, so far as known, this plant does not occur at the Cape, it is quite possible that he brought this specimen from India or China, and confounded all those plants under one name. He does not mention *C. Chinensis* or any other *Cuscuta* from those regions.

C. nitida seems to be one of the commonest species at the Cape of Good Hope, and has been collected there by almost every botanist. Dr. R. C. Alexander communicated a specimen with firmer red stems; some of Drege's specimens exhibit a granulated, somewhat scabrous, calyx.

18. C. AFRICANA, Thunberg? Fl. Cap. 568 & Phyt. Bl. 17; Choisy! Cusc. 176 & DC. Prod. IX. 454 pro parte.—I have above stated my doubts about the identity of Thunberg's plant, and my reasons, nevertheless, for retaining his name for this species. The older botanists also seem to acknowledge this for *C. Africana,* as I find a specimen, thus labeled, in Willdenow's Herb. nro. 3161. Choisy's description entirely refers to this plant, though one of the specimens, he cites, belongs to *C. angulata.*

It is well characterized by the very loose inflorescence, the long pedicels, the capillary styles which are much longer (often more than twice as long), than the oblong and thick divergent stigmata; calyx short, lobes broad, obtusish, verrucose, imbricate; laciniæ linear-oblong, obtusish, involute at the margin and at tip, erect or spreading; scales large, often longer than the tube, incurved; capsules in the only specimen, in which I could find any, almost baccate, or opening very late, with the corolla persistent at base, mostly with a

single globose seed, 0.7 lines long; flower 1–1½ lines long.—
C. Americana, Thunb. Prod. 32, not of Linnæus, is the same
as his later *C. Africana*.—Our plant was collected by Drege!
7010 and labeled by him *C. Africana, d;* it is Ecklon & Zeyher's! 22, 70, 10. *Schrebera schinoides*, Lin. sp. 1662, is, as
the figure in Nov. Act. Ups. I. t. 5, f. 1, shows, this species,
parasitic on *Myrica Africana*. *C. fusiformis*, Willd. rel. in
R. & S. VI. 209, referred here by Choisy, a misprint for *C.
funiformis*, as spelt in Willd. Herb. nro. 3156, is not a *Cuscuta* but a *Cassyta* from the Cape, as Schlechtendal has long
since stated.

   C. Capensis, Choisy! Cusc. 175 t. 1, f. 4, and DC. Prod. IX.
454, is a large form of this species; flowers 2¼–2¾ lines long,
calyx smoother and shorter, laciniæ longer, somewhat acutish, scales smaller; it bears the same relation to *C. Africana*
that *C. Trifolii* does to *C. Epithymum*.—Drege! 7833, Dr.
Thom! Dr Alexander!

Sec. 5.   *Eugrammica.*

   Styles of unequal length, subulate or cylindric; stigmata
capitate.   Capsule bursting transversely more or less regularly; in *C. Jalapensis* regularly circumscissile.   Seeds often
only one or two in each capsule, rounded or flattened, truncate at base, or hooked; hilum forming a transverse or oblique,
rarely a perpendicular line, often very short, or reduced to a
point.

   The inflorescence is quite variable, forming few-flowered
loose cymes, or compound racemose or umbelliform cymes
with pedicelled flowers, or compact clusters with subsessile
flowers; with bracts at the base of each or at least the prima-
ry pedicels or flowers.   The corolla remains at the base or on
the top of the capsule or completely envelops it.

   Most species of this section inhabit South America, the
West Indies, and Mexico; one (*C. umbellata*) extends into
the southwestern parts of the United States, and two (*C.
odontolepis* and *C. applanata*) are peculiar to that region;
two others are natives of Asia, one extending to New Holland, the other to eastern Africa.

§ 1.   Subulatæ.

   Styles thick and short, subulate from a broad base; flowers mostly
large and of a firm texture; scales wanting in one (the first) species;
corolla enveloping the whole or the greater part of the ripe capsule in all
but the first; capsule opening readily by more or less regular circumscission.

19. C. GRANDIFLORA, Humb. Bonpl. Kunth! n. gen. sp. III. 123, t. 213; DC. Prod. IX. 457; not Wallich Cat. —This beautiful and striking species is so well described by Kunth that it is not necessary to add a single line. He already mentions (as he also does in regard to *C. Popayanensis*) the circumscissile opening of the capsule, ignored by later writers. The *raceme* of flowers on the left side of his otherwise very correct figure is imaginary, as the inflorescence is a loose few-flowered cyme. The flowers have a diameter of full 4 lines, and are 2½–3 lines high; the subulate filaments are inserted a little below the throat; no trace of scales visible; styles and capsule scabrous or verrucose; dry corolla at base of capsule; ripe seeds only 0.8 lines in diameter, almost globose, very rough; hilum a mere dot.

This species is peculiar to the Andes about the Equator; New Granada, Humboldt! Purdie! Goudot! Peru, Haenke! Cl. Gay! Weddell! 4768; Bolivia, Weddell! 4518; Chili, Edmonston!

20. C. ODORATA, Ruiz & Pavon! Fl. Peruv. I. 69, t. 105, f. a., not Choisy nor Pœppig; *C. intermedia*, Choisy! Cusc. 179, t. 2, f. 3 and DC. Prod. IX. 455; Gay, Fl. Chil. IV. 447.— After examining the original specimen in Hb. Ruiz, now in the royal Herbarium at Berlin, and the almost identical one in Hb. Pavon, now in the possession of E. Boissier of Geneva, which latter is the original for Choisy's description, I can have no doubt about the identity of these plants.—Flowers 3 lines long, 3–4 lines in diameter, on very short pedicels, forming dense lateral clusters; laciniæ rather longer than the shallow tube; scales very large, deeply fringed; corolla surrounding and partly covering the irregularly circumscissile capsule; seeds triangular-rounded, nearly one line long.—In the Flora Peruviana the capsule is already figured as circumscissile; but the whole figure, especially the details, are not very correct, and rather calculated to mislead.

Peru, Ruiz! Pavon! A. Matthews! 486; Weddell! 4693; Ecuador, Seemann! 852; Chili, Cl. Gay! 38 & 815.—In Weddell's specimen the tube is more cylindrical and longer and the lobes rather shorter, uniting this species with

Var. *β.* ? BOTRYOIDES, from southern Brazil, Lobb! 49, in the Kew Herbarium.—Dense clusters of flowers arranged in long pendulous bunches, resembling grapes; tube deeply campanulate, almost cylindric, nearly twice as long as the broad, rounded laciniæ; corolla enveloping the widely gaping capsule, the styles of which are shorter and thicker than in *C. odorata;* stylar portion of dissepiment broad and jagged.—

Apparently intermediate between this and *C. Chilensis*, and perhaps specifically distinct.

21. C. JALAPENSIS, Schlechtendal! Linnæa VIII. p. 515. —Though well and carefully described, and published as early as 1833, this well marked species has been overlooked by later writers. It is similar to the last, but much smaller; flowers, though on short pedicels, much less crowded; its most striking character consists in the regularly circumscissile conic capsule, with shorter very strongly subulate styles, whence Schlechtendal not inappropriately calls it " bicornis." Peculiar to Mexico; Jalapa, Schiede! 152; Linden! 308; near Mexico, Graham! 250; Bustamente! 83; Oaxaca, Galeotti! 4413.

22. C. CHILENSIS, Ker, Bot. Reg. VII. f. 603; Choisy! in DC. Prod. IX. 455; Gay! Fl. Chil. IV. 446; *C. odorata*, Pœppig! in Hb. 90.—A common plant in Chili, whence almost every collector sends it; well characterized by the densely clustered almost sessile flowers, cylindric tube, large, linear, almost sessile anthers, and short deeply fringed scales; styles as long as the irregularly circumscissile capsule, even in fruit scarcely reaching to the throat of the tube; seed oval, triangular, compressed, 0.7–0.8 lines long, with a small umbilicus marked with radiating lines, which centre in the small round hilum.

** Lobes of calyx acute.

23. C. FŒTIDA, Humb. Bonpl. Kunth.! n. gen. sp. III. 122; DC. Prod. IX. 460; not Hook. & Arn. Bot. Beechy; *C. pycnantha*, Bentham! Pl. Hartw. p. 226; *C. corymbosa*, Jussieu! in Hb. Juss.—Clusters large and compact, ½–1 inch in diameter, flowers fully 3 lines long; lobes of calyx and of cylindrical corolla very acute or acuminate; stamens very short; scales much shorter than the tube, in Humbolt's specimen broadly oval, in others narrow; styles strongly subulate, as long as capsule; seeds 0.6 lines long. Quito, 8,000 to 10,000 feet high, Humboldt! Couthouy! Peru, Jos. Jussieu!, Ecuador, Seemann! Columbia, Hartweg! 1238.

24. C. ACUTILOBA, n. sp.: caule filiformi; cymis laxis paucifloris; pedicellis brevibus bracteis lanceolatis acuminatis suffultis; calycis campanulati lobis triangulatis acutis tubum corollæ profunde campanulatum æquantibus; laciniis lanceolatis acutissimis erectis demum reflexis tubum æquantibus seu paulo longioribus; staminibus multo brevioribus, filamentis anthera ovata brevioribus; squamis spatulatis fimbriatis faucem fere æquantibus; stylis e basi crassa subulatis ovarium

æquantibus inclusis ; capsula corolla marcescente tota involuta irregulariter circumscissa.

At the bridge of Obragilla, Peru, Alex. Matthews! 661 in Hb. Hooker.—Very nearly allied to the last, distinguished by the loose few-flowered inflorescence, the small and apparently deep purple (a color not noticed in any other species) flowers, the triangular, not imbricate, lobes, the short tube of the corolla and the still more broadly subulate styles ; by the styles it is distinguished from *C. umbellata*, which it otherwise considerably resembles.—Flowers 1¼–1½ lines long; single seeds globose.

§ 2 Obtusilobæ.

Styles slender, usually capillary; flowers large or small, usually thin and membranaceous ; lobes of calyx obtuse in all but the last species ; corolla short in the 3 first, long and cylindric with short laciniæ in the 4 last species ; scales absent in one (the last) species ; styles short in the first, very long in the 4 last species ; capsule opening late and mostly irregularly ; dead corolla enveloping the capsule except in the first species.

* Flowers short.

25. C. APPLANATA, n. sp.: caule filiformi; floribus breviter pedicellatis vel subsessilibus in glomerulos densos sæpe continuos congestis; calycis campanulati tenuis lobis ovatis obtusis tubum corollæ late campanulatum depressum æquantibus; laciniis ovatis obtusis patulis demum reflexis tubo æquilongis; antheris oblongis filamenta brevia subulata æquantibus; squamis maximis crispato-laciniatis faucem excedentibus supra ovarium magnum depressum incurvis; stylis capillaribus ovarium æquantibus seu excedentibus e fauce exsertis; capsula depressa corolla marcescente involuta irregulariter circumscissa.

In Arizona Territory south of the Gila River, Chs. Wright! Mex. Bound. Survey, 1623 (541) on some *Nyctaginea* and 1625 (685) on *Ambrosia*; fl. Sept.—Glomerules 3–4 lines in diameter, often strung together like beads; 6–12 flowers in each glomerule, 1–1½ lines long, of thin texture and white color, on short branched pedicels, supported by small obtuse bracts; capsule 1 line in diameter, half as much in height, with a very small intrastylar opening; seeds ½ line long, oval, strongly verrucose-reticulate, with a short and broad oblique or perpendicular hilum. In aspect this plant resembles somewhat *C. arvensis*, but is abundantly distinct from this and any other species.

26. C. CHINENSIS, Lamarck! Enc. II. 229; Choisy! Cusc. 183, t. 3, f. 4 and DC. Prod. IX. 457; *C. sulcata*, Roxb. Ind. I. 447; Wallich! Cat. 1320²; *C. capillaris*, Wall.! Cat. 1321; *C. Americana*, Thunberg! in Hb. Jussieu; *Grammica aphylla*,

Loureiro! Cochin. 171; ed. Willd. I. 212.—A common plant, as it appears, of the tropical regions of Asia, and the islands southward, especially Ceylon, extending into Candahar (Griffith! 685) and China (in Hb. H. B. Petropol! as " *C. fimbriata*, Bunge," which name seems to be apocryphal), characterized by the strongly carinate rather than sulcate lobes of the thereby 5-angled calyx, with 5 secondary angles at the commissures; scales rather large, deeply laciniate, and not, as Choisy describes and figures them, short and adnate below the throat; styles slender; capsule very thin, enveloped and covered by the corolla, opening at base rather irregularly and late, and therefore often termed "baccate;" Loureiro himself describes the fruit of his genus *Grammica* as a "bacca," though his original specimen in the Hb. of the British Museum shows the circumscissile capsule. Flowers 1–1$\frac{1}{4}$ lines long; seeds 0.5–0.7 lines long, oval; hilum oblique or usually nearly perpendicular.—Lamarck's original specimen, accidentally raised in the Jardin des Plantes of Paris, in 1784, with seeds supposed to have come from China, is preserved in Hb. Jussieu in Mus. Paris.

C. hyalina, Wight, ic. 1372; Wallich! Cat. 1320[1], not Roth, is a form of this species with bifid and rather small scales.

A form from the island of Nassibé, near Madagascar, Boivin! in Hb. Vindobon., has also bifid scales, but is distinguished from all other varieties by the capsule being exsert above the corolla and by the large intrastylar aperture.

Var. β. CARINATA; *C. carinata*, R. Brown! Prod. N. Holl. I. 491, from the tropical parts of New Holland, is the same species with more strongly carinate and more obtuse lobes of the calyx, more obtuse laciniæ and almost globose anthers.

Var. γ. CILIARIS; *C. ciliaris*, Hohenacker! in Pl. Kotschy, Boissier! diag. or. II. 3, 129, is a stouter, larger flowered northern form of the same plant, with shorter and stouter styles; scales spatulate, or sometimes in the same flower bifid, less deeply and finely fimbriate; flowers 1$\frac{3}{4}$–2$\frac{1}{4}$ lines long.— Mossul, Kotschy! 431; Kurdistan, Grant! in Hb. Torrey.— The specimen of Herb. Wight. propr.! 2408, is the same thing from India. The largest flowered form is preserved in Hb. Mus. Paris, under the name of *C. exigua*, collected at the Selenga river, in Siberia, by Demidoff, a cotemporary of Pallas; lobes of calyx and corolla, in this specimen, more distinctly crenulate than in most other forms of the species.

27. C. TINCTORIA, Martius! in Herb.: caulibus filiformibus subfunicularibus; floribus globosis pedicellatis in glomerulos laxos umbelliformes congestis; calycis cupulati lobis orbiculatis imbricatis tubum corollæ campanulatum æquantibus;

laciniis tubo æquilongis ovatis obtusis basi imbricatis erectis
seu demum patulis reflexive; antheris ovatis filamento subulato brevissimo plerumque longioribus; squamis late-ovatis
fimbriato-laceris tubum æquantibus seu paulo excedentibus
incurvis; stylis filiformibus ovario depresso longioribus fere
exsertis; capsula irregulariter circumscissa corolla marcescente involuta tectaque.

Mexico, usually, as it seems, on trees: Oaxaca on *Schinus
molle*, Karwinski! who relates that the natives use it under the name of "Zaca-tlascalli" as a yellow dye; and, indeed, the dried specimens tinge water, paper, etc., deep yellow, which I notice also in some other South American *Cuscutæ;* San Luis Potosi, on the same species of tree, Dr.
Gregg! in full bloom in December.—Flowers 2–2½ lines
long, in loose clusters, of 6 lines in diameter, which are
gathered into long racemes; intrastylar aperture small;
seed compressed, rounded, 0.6 lines in diameter.—The slender style and the shape of the capsule distinguish this species from the similar *C. Jalapensis*, the short flower and short
style from *C. floribunda*, the circumscissile capsule and larger
flower from *C. Gronovii*, and the short filaments from all of
them; a specimen, however, in the Hb. H. Bot. of St. Petersburg, collected by Karwinski on an oak "between Victo-
ria and the Rio Blanco" has filaments as long as the anthers.

** Flowers elongated.

✝ 28. C. FLORIBUNDA, Humb. Bonpl. Kunth! n. gen. sp. III.
123; DC. Prod. IX. 459.—The only specimens of this plant,
known to me, gathered by Bonpland! at the bridge of Istla,
in western Mexico, 3000 feet high, are preserved in the royal
Hb. at Berlin and in Hb. Willdenow, nro. 3159³; they are
in rather poor condition, and in ripe fruit only; enough is left,
however, to show that the plant is nearly allied to *C. Popayanensis* as Kunth already states, but well distinguished by the
short and thick, orbicular, deeply divided, broadly imbricate
lobes of the calyx, the deeply divided corolla; the oblong
linear (obtuse, not acute, as Kunth has it) laciniæ nearly
equalling in length the cylindric tube; large oval scales deeply
fimbriate-laciniate, reaching to the throat; styles twice as
long as capsule, slender, long exsert in fruit; stylar portion
of dissepiment elongated, almost reaching the base of the
capsule; seed 0.8 lines long, narrow, triangular and very
rough. Flower with the lobes 3, or, when these are reflexed,
2 lines long. From *C. tinctoria*, to which it is even more
closely allied, it may be distinguished by the long tube, the
narrow laciniæ, the long styles, and the long and narrow
seeds.

29. C. AMERICANA, Lin. sp. 180 pro parte; Jacq. Am. 30, p. 17; Choisy! Cusc. 186, t. 4, f. 4; DC. Prod. IX. 459.— This is the most common species of the West Indian Islands, parasitic mostly on shrubs and trees; it extends to the Pacific coast of Mexico, and on the Atlantic coast of South America from Venezuela to Brazil, rarely, as it would seem, leaving the neighborhood of the sea coast; though Weddell found it in the province of Goyaz in central Brazil.—Well characterized by the small, cylindric corolla, with short, very obtuse, almost always erect laciniæ slightly protruding over, or sometimes almost enclosed by, the wide and deep, cupulate calyx; scales short, attached to the middle of the corolla and usually not reaching to its throat; styles very slender, mostly much longer than the very small globose ovary, exsert only in fruit; capsule late and irregularly circumscissile; stylar portion of dissepiment reaching nearly to the base of the capsule; seeds mostly solitary, filling the whole capsule, roundish, somewhat compressed; hilum forming a very short line, almost a point.

The ordinary C. Americana has flowers 1¼–1½ lines in length; a thin, when dry, membranaceous and very wide calyx; scales either truncate, sometimes almost bilobed, slightly dentate, or somewhat fimbriate; styles usually included during flowering, more or less exsert in fruit.—Martinique, Sieber! 91; Hayti, Poiteau! Ehrenberg! Antigua, Wullschlægel! with larger flowers; Portorico, Bertero! St. Thomas, Ridlé! Holton! Yucatan, Linden! Venezuela, Humboldt! Karsten! Fendler! 2069; Surinam, Hb. Ac. Phil.! Brazil, Gardner! 1775; Blanchet! 736; Goyaz, Weddell! 2208.

Different varieties may be distinguished according to the length of the pedicels, size of flower, texture of calyx, shape of scales and length of styles, but they run into one another so that I, with 25 or 30 specimens from the whole range of the species before me, am unable to limit even these varieties. The smallest form is C. congesta, Bentham! Bot. Sulph. 138, from Acapulco; flowers crowded; scarcely more than 1 line long; scales triangular, almost entire; styles slender. A similar plant was collected by Dr. Gregg at Mazatlan; flowers rather more slender, calyx narrower than in any other form, and more distinctly 5-angled (angles corresponding to the commissures); scales and styles as in the other. C. leiolepis, Miquel! Linnæa XVIII. 247, is the same thing from the orange hedges in Surinam, but with shorter styles than any other form of this species, examined by me. C. Surinamensis, Schilling, de Lepra p. 60 & 200, t. 2, also seems to belong here. C. campanulata, Nuttall! Mss. in Hb. Ac. Phil. from the West Indies, has the scales of this, but otherwise is identical with the ordinary form.

Another form has a thicker, more coriaceous calyx, usually larger flowers ($1\frac{1}{2}$–$2\frac{1}{4}$ lines long), larger more deeply fimbriate scales, often exsert styles, and sometimes two-seeded capsules. This is *C. spectabilis*, Choisy! Cusc. 187, t. 5, f. 1; DC. Prod. IX. 459, from Bahia, Salzmann! 351; Blanchet! 85, and *C. globulosa*, Bentham! Bot. Sulph. 138, from Acapulco; the specimens from Surinam, Hostmann! 464, one of Poiteau's! from Hayti, and especially Linden! 1994, from Cuba, the largest of all, may be referred here.

C. Americana, Lin. and of most authors on the Flora of North America, comprises besides this several North American species, especially *C. Gronovii, C. arvensis* and *C. compacta. C. Americana*, Thunb. is *C. Africana*.

— 30. C. CORYMBOSA, Ruiz & Pavon, as intended by the authors, is a rare form of a species which under different names is common throughout northern South America and Mexico. The species, as here proposed, is distinguished by the cupulate membranaceous calyx, with short and broad very obtuse lobes, loosely enclosing the lower part of the long cylindric tube of the corolla; laciniæ short, mostly very obtuse, erect or rarely spreading; anthers oval or orbicular-oval, sessile or on very short filaments; scales mostly long and narrow, attached for the greater part of their length, more or less fringed at the sides and apex, always considerably shorter than the tube, rarely quite small and indistinct; ovary small, globular or conic, with very long styles, which generally reach as high as the anthers, and often become exsert as the fruit ripens; capsule very small, often 1-seeded, always opening in its largest diameter, surrounded and covered by the base of the shrivelled corolla; stylar portion of dissepiment reaching nearly to the bottom of the capsule; hilum reduced to a point. Very closely allied to the last species but readily distinguished by the larger flowers, and the larger elongated and exsert corolla.

Var. *a*. GRANDIFLORA: flowers large, 3–4 lines long; anthers on very short filaments or sessile; scales long and narrow, almost entirely adnate, rarely bifid; styles reaching the anthers or shorter; ovary and capsule globose or rarely somewhat conic. *C. Popayanensis*, H. B. K.! n. gen. sp. III. 123; DC. Prod. IX. 460, of which Kunth already mentions the capsule as circumscissile, and speaks of the close alliance to *C. corymbosa; C. cymosa*, Willd.! rel. R. & Sch. VI. 205, founded on the same specimen.—New Granada, Humboldt! Columbia, Hartweg! 1237; Moritz! 489; Comitan, Mexico, Linden! 291; Carracas, Birchel! Gollmer! Venezuela, Fendler! 946; Peru, Dombey! in Hb. Mus. Paris, under the name of *C. corymbosa*.

The following forms do not seem sufficiently distinct from

this: *C. patens*, Benth.! Bot. Sulph. 35, from the Magdalen Bay, Lower California, has rather wider and a little shorter flowers and shorter styles, which reach only as high as the linear scales.

C. inclusa, Choisy! Cusc. 179, t. 2, f. 2; DC. Prod. IX. 455, from Mexico, Berlandier! 1103; similar to the last, styles even longer, but scarcely reaching the throat; anthers sessile. Choisy's figure shows long filaments and his description speaks of "stamina basi corollæ affixa," etc., which is perfectly unintelligible. Choisy's figures are by no means reliable in the details, as is evident in examining, for example, the scales in his figures of *C. Arabica*, *Chinensis* and others, the ovary of *C. Gronovii*, *Americana*, etc. This is one of the few *Cuscutæ* known to me, where there is in the flower in full bloom a slight approach to the ventricose shape.

C. laxiflora, Benth.! Bot. Sulph. 138, from Acapulco, is the same plant, with a somewhat conic ovary and capsule, uniting this with the next form; flowers about 3 lines long, styles not exsert.

C. Popayanensis, Pœppig! Hb. is a variety of *C. micrantha*.

Var. β. STYLOSA; *C. stylosa*, Choisy! Cusc. 187, t. 5, f. 2; DC. Prod. IX. 459.—Flowers rarely more than 2 lines long, slender, with very short calyx; narrow cylindric corolla; short, narrow scales; filaments as long or shorter than anthers; styles reaching to the throat of the corolla or above it, often long exert at maturity of fruit or before; ovary and capsule conic or rather inversely pear-shaped. The length of the styles is variable, even in the original specimens, quoted by Choisy; the shape of the capsule would be characteristic enough, if intermediate forms did not indicate a transition to var. *grandiflora*.—Found, thus far, only in Mexico: Andrieux! 73 and 214; Berlandier! 822; Hb. Jacquin! under the name of *C. Americana*; Ghiesbrecht! 186; Toluca, Karwinski! Zimapan, Galeotti! 1412; Jalapa, Linden! 308 in part.

In the Kew Herbarium I find a specimen sent by Botteri from the Orizaba, Mexico (nro. 949), which is this form with scarcely exsert styles, larger flowers (3 lines long) and acutish crenulate laciniæ.

Var. γ. MICROLEPIS; *C. corymbosa*, Ruiz & Pavon! Fl. Peruv. I. 69, t. 105, b., not Choisy Cusc. nor DC. Prod.—Flowers 1¾–2 lines long, as often 5 as 4 parted in the original specimens in Hb. Ruiz and in Hb. Pavon, both of which seem to be parts of one and the same specimen; calyx cupulate with short obtuse lobes, half as long as the corolla; laciniæ ovate, obtuse, nearly one-third the length of the tube, erect or patulous; filaments as long as the broadly ovate-cordate anthers; scales reduced to very thin and small ovate membranes, with 4-7 or 8 irregular teeth, inserted below the middle of the tube; perhaps sometimes entirely wanting; ovary slightly conic, with styles scarcely reaching to the throat, just exsert in fruit. In the figure in the Flora Peruviana the cylindric corolla and the circumscissile capsule are correctly given.—Peru, on shrubs, and on *Medicago sativa,* Ruiz & Pavon! not found since.

It is well known that Choisy, l. c. and every author after him, myself included, took the *Cuscuta,* which twenty years ago made its appearance in different parts of Europe, in fields of *Medicago,* said to have been imported from Chili, for this species. The figure, as well as the original specimens, prove this to have been a mistake; that plant is *C. racemosa* Mart., as will be shown below. Whether the scales are ever really absent, or only very small and difficult to find, I can not say; in 8 or 10 flowers, which I carefully examined, I could not always discover them, especially after soaking the flowers; unfortunately the specimens are injured by too hard pressing. With the exception of the smaller flowers and indistinct scales, I find nothing to separate this from the other forms, which are more abundant and better developed, but had to yield their specific names to priority.

31. C. PRISMATICA, Pavon! Mss.; Choisy! Cusc.182, t. 3, f. 2; DC. Prod. IX. 457.—A very distinct species, and one of the few without any scales. Choisy's figure as well as description is not very correct. Bracts lanceolate acuminate; flowers subsessile, 3 lines long; calyx elongated, obconic, fleshy, deep red, 5-angled from the decurrent carinæ of the unequal, ovate, acute or cuspidate imbricate lobes; corolla almost cylindric, long exsert, externally granulated, laciniæ 4-6 times shorter than the tube, oblong, obtuse, somewhat involute at the margins, crenulate; anthers ovate-cordate, sessile; ovary turbinate; capillary styles shorter than the tube, much longer than the ovary. I have seen no fruit of this plant, but venture to class it here on account of its close affinity with the last species, from which however it is abundantly distinguished by all the characters above enumerated.

The only specimens seen are from Guayaquil, Pavon! in Hb. Boissier, and Hænke! in Hb. Mus. Bohem. Pr.

§ 3. *Leptolobæ.*

Styles slender, usually capillary; flowers rather small, membranaceous; lobes of calyx and corolla acute, often acuminate, commonly narrow and elongated, as long or longer than the usually campanulate tube; scales absent only in the last species; capsule surrounded or covered by the corolla, opening by irregular or rather regular circumscission.

X   32. C. ODONTOLEPIS, n. sp.: caulibus tenuiter filiformibus; floribus breviter pedicellatis bracteatis in glomerulos laxiores demum decompositos crassos confertis; calycis breviter campanulati profunde partiti nitidi lobis ovato-triangulatis acutiusculis tubum corollæ profunde campanulatum subæquantibus; laciniis ovato-lanceolatis acutis demum patulis reflexisve tubo paulo brevioribus; antheris ovatis filamenta subulata brevia æquantibus; squamis late ovatis e tubi basi oriundis ad medium adnatis faucem fere attingentibus versus apicem grosse dentatis; stylis capillaceis ovario depresso-globoso multoties longioribus e fauce paulo exsertis demum elongatis; capsula corollæ rudimentis calyptrata rite circumscissa.

Near a deserted Rancho on a rocky hill side in Arizona, parasitic on Amarantus; fl. Sept., Chs. Wright! 1624 (529).—"Whole plant very white." Clusters of the large and showy flowers at last crowded, more than 1 inch in diameter; flowers 2½ lines long, on pedicels as long or shorter than the calyx, which in one specimen covers the tube, and in another is shorter; scales large, irregularly toothed towards the apex only; capsule globose; readily opening towards the base by a small circular aperture; stylar portion of dissepiment scarcely half as long as capsule; seeds usually all 4 developed; oval, about ½ line long, verrucose, with a small, linear, vertical or transverse hilum.—In general aspect as well as in some particulars this species very closely approaches to C. corymbosa, but seems to be well distinguished by the characters given, especially the deeply divided corolla, its acute laciniæ, the broad dentate scales, the small basal opening of the capsule, the seed, etc.; it is not impossible, however, that intermediate forms may yet be discovered, which will oblige a future monographer to unite them. On the other hand, the similarity to C. subinclusa, a Californian species, which has decidedly baccate capsules, is so great, that one might be induced to doubt the diagnostic importance of this character.

33. C. XANTHOCHORTOS, Martius! in Hb.: caulibus filiformibus; glomerulis sessilibus globosis multifloris; bracteis ovatis; pedicellis ramosis, ultimis calyce campanulato profunde fisso brevioribus; lobis ovatis obtusis basi imbricatis margine sæpe reflexis tubum corollæ late campanulatum æquantibus seu superantibus; laciniis lanceolatis elongatis acutiusculis tubo multo longioribus patulis reflexisve basi imbricatis; antheris oblongis filamento subulato subbrevioribus; squamis late ovatis fimbriato-laceris faucem excedentibus; stylis capillaceis demum divaricatis ovario ovato multo longioribus; capsula conica corollæ rudimento involuta basi regulariter circumscissa.

Porto Alegre, Rio Grande de San Pedro, Brazil, Father Joannes de Sta. Barbara! in Hb. Martius.—The specimen consists of an intricate mass of deep yellow stems with few heads of flowers just developing; a few half ripe, but already circumscissile fruits were seen. Flowers 1½–2 lines long. This plant seems to be nearly allied to *C. umbellata*, but is distinguished by more compact heads, larger flowers, broad and imbricate obtusish lobes, etc. The laciniæ of the corolla, always elongated, are in some flowers acutish, in others almost obtuse.

34. C. PARTITA, Choisy! Cusc. 188, t. 5, f. 3; DC. Prod. IX. 460.—Brazil, Blanchet! 3047; Gardner! 2684; westward to Bolivia, Weddell! 3483 and 3611, and northward to Venezuela, Maracaibo, Karsten! and Curaçao, Friedrichsthal! 375, b; usually low, on herbaceous plants, *Leguminosæ*, *Malvaceæ*, *Euphorbiaceæ*, etc.—Cymes compound, paniculate; bracts ovate lanceolate, often crenate; flowers small, usually less than 1 line long, more or less glandulous and filled with coloring matter, deep-red, when dry, like *C. miniata;* calyx divided almost to the base, lobes lanceolate acute; lobes of corolla of same shape, at length reflexed with the points incurved; tube of corolla at last ventricose, enveloping the capsule, divided by grooves which correspond to the stamens into 5 separate externally convex compartments as it were; scales as long as the tube or shorter, deeply fringed; capillary styles much longer than the small globose ovary, subexert, sometimes recurved on the fruit; capsule very thin, hyaline, irregularly circumscissile with a wide opening; seeds 0.5–0.6 lines long, obliquely ovate, or, where only one in a cell is developed, rostrate; hilum linear-oblong, short, in the former seeds perpendicular, in the latter transverse.

The specimens from Bolivia have larger, less glandulous, and paler flowers, 1¼–1½ lines long, "yellowish-white or rose-colored," but do not differ in any other respect.

35. C. UMBELLATA, Humb. Bonp. Kunth! n. gen. sp. III. 121; DC. Prod. IX. 460; *C. parviflora*, Willd.! Hb. nro. 3163. This species seems to have been unknown to all later botanists with the exception of Torrey, who recognized Humboldt's plant in a specimen collected by Long's expedition to the Rocky Mountains. Lately it has turned up from many localities along the United States and Mexican boundary line, from northern Mexico and from the Antilles; in Brazil a form has been collected which I can not specifically distinguish from the Mexican plant.—The flowers of this species are arranged in loose compound fasciculate cymes, the ultimate divisions forming umbells of 3-5-7 flowers supported by a single ovate-lanceolate bract; pedicels usually longer than the flower; flower, with the lobes of the corolla erect, 1½–2 lines long; calyx broadly campanulate, thin and shining, at least when dry; lobes triangular, acute, as long or longer

than the shallow tube of the corolla; laciniæ narrowly lanceolate, elongate, acute, longer than the tube, spreading or reflexed; scales usually broadly oval, large, longer than the tube, incurved; styles much longer than the globose-depressed ovary, rarely of same length; corolla enveloping the small thin depressed, almost 4-lobed capsule, which is commonly circumscissile, but in some instances rather irregularly bursting; seeds generally all 4 developed, 0.5–0.6 lines long, triangular, oblique, with a very short linear hilum.

It is always found in dry places on low herbs, especially *Portulacca*, also *Kallstræmia, Amarantus, Atriplex, Polygonum*, etc., and sometimes even on some prostrate *Euphorbiæ*: between Queretaro and Salamanca, Humboldt! Saltillo and Camargo, Gregg! Western Texas, New Mexico and Arizona, Wright! 1627, 1636, 1639 (371, 510, 695), Bigelow! Schott! Santa Fé, Fendler! 659; foot of the Rocky Mountains, James! Jamaica, Broomfield! Purdie!

Dr. Hays found a specimen on the San Pedro River, Arizona, on *Suæda*, with much more dense inflorescence, greatly resembling a form of *C. Californica*, which will be noticed below, parasitic on the same saline plant, and mainly distinguished by the broadly campanulate, not turbinate, calyx, the circumscissile capsule and the seeds.

Some specimens from New Mexico show a tendency to papillose pubescence, and one from Sonora, Coulter! 1010, on some *Euphorbia*, has the unusually small flowers (1 line long) quite papillose-scabrous.

Var. *β. ?* DESERTORUM; *C. Desertorum*, Martius! in Hb.; pedicels long, flowers less crowded, smaller, 1 line long; lanceolate-linear laciniæ twice as long as tube; scales small, bifid or reduced to two lateral toothed lobes; styles shorter than the exsert capsule, which is circumscissile with a small opening; intrastylar aperture large; seeds only 0.4 line long.— On *Portulacca* and *Ehrenbergia* in the province of Piauhy, Brazil, Martius!—Another similar form, but with longer tube and shorter laciniæ and rather larger scales, was collected by Gardner! 2425, in the province of Ceara in the same neighborhood, also on *Portulacca*.

A specimen from the island of Antigua in Hb. Martius, Wullschlægel! 352, seems to belong here, though the (unripe) capsules do not open; flowers larger and more densely clustered than in the common form, calyx and capsule glandulous, intrastylar aperture large.

36. C. GRACILLIMA, n. sp.: caulibus tenuissime capillaceis demum deciduis; floribus in fasciculos decompositos demum dense glomeratos congestis; bracteis lineari-lanceolatis; pedunculis ramosissimis; pedicellis capillaceis flore gracili longioribus; calycis turbinati lobis lanceolatis sæpe apice recurvis

tubum corollæ paulo superantibus; laciniis lanceolatis subulatis tubo multo longioribus erectis apice subrecurvis; staminibus lacinias superantibus, filamentis e basi subulata capillaceis, antheris ovatis; squamis laceris fimbriatis incurvis tubum excedentibus; ovario parvo globoso, stylis capillaceis longissimis antheras fere attingentibus; capsula corollæ rudimento indusiata demum irregulariter transverse disrupta; seminibus lenticularibus læviusculis.—*C. fœtida*, Hook. & Arn.! Bot. Beechy, 304, non H. B. K.; *C. subtilis*, Chaubard! in Hb.

Mexico, Mornay! in Hb. Delessert; Tepic, Beechy! in Hb. Hooker; Jürgensen! in Hb. Mus. Florent.—The only species known to me with stamens longer than the lobes of the corolla; distinguished also by the large and dense masses (in one specimen over 1 inch thick and 2–3 inches long) of flowers; pedicels branched but scarcely umbellate, mostly much longer than the flowers; flowers small and slender, $1\frac{1}{4}$–$1\frac{1}{2}$ lines long; capsule opening late and irregularly; intrastylar aperture quite small; seeds usually two, 0.5 line long, compressed, rounded, slightly oblique at base, with a very short transverse or oblique hilum.—Closely allied to *C. umbellata*, principally distinguished by the inflorescence, the turbinate calyx, the smoothish seed; less important differences are the erect laciniæ and long filaments.

Var. *β*. SACCHARATA: bracteis pedicellis totoque flore papilloso-adspersis; laciniis staminibus stylisque brevioribus; seminibus minoribus.—*C. Sidarum*, Liebm.! in Hb.

On the coast of Oaxaca, parasitic on different species of *Sida*, Liebmann! in Hb. Hooker.—Inflorescence the same as in the species, flowers even smaller, $1\frac{1}{4}$ lines long, laciniæ shorter, stamens shorter, anthers orbicular, capsule readily circumscissile, seeds 0.4 line long.

✕ 37. C. LEPTANTHA, n. sp.: caulibus capillaceis; bracteis ovatis acuminatis; pedicellis filiformibus lævibus umbellato-fasciculatis; floribus 4-meris gracilibus; calycis granulato-hispidi lobis triangulatis acutis tubo corollæ cylindrico dimidio brevioribus; laciniis lanceolatis acutis erecto-patulis tubo multo brevioribus; filamentis filiformibus cum antheris ovatis brevioribus lacinias subæquantibus; squamis ovatis dentato-fimbriatis tubo multo brevioribus; ovario parvo globoso, stylis capillaribus longissimis demum exsertis; capsula corollæ basi hispidula indusiata calyptrataque circumscissa; seminibus globoso-triangulatis verruculosis.

Western Texas, Chs. Wright! 1849, nro. 522; prairies of the Leona, in the same region, the same! 1852, nro. 1639 in part (mixed with *C. umbellata*), in both instances on *Euphorbia albo-marginata*.—This is the only *Cuscuta* seen by me with (thus far) constantly 4-parted flowers. Flowers 2–$2\frac{1}{4}$ lines long, pedicels sometimes twice as long; calyx campanulate-globose, short in proportion, about ¾ line long, as well as the base of the tube in all the specimens seen, papillose or, in the dry plant, scabrous; tube of the corolla slender, much longer than calyx; corolla enveloping the small capsule and contracted above it, capsule readily opening at base with a wide aperture; seeds 2–4, almost globose, 0.4 line long, with a very short hilum.

38. C. HYALINA, Roth! nov. spec. p. 100, not Wight, nor Boissier; *C. Arabica*, Wight, ic. t. 1371, not Fresenius; *C. oxypetala*, Boissier! diag. or. II. 3, 130; *C. acutissima*, Buchinger! Mss. in Pl. Schimper.—This well marked species of the tropical parts of the East Indies (Heyne! Stocks! 478; Hooker & Thomson! and others), extending into Abyssinia (Schimper! 1522) is certainly the plant Roth had in view, as the specimens with Heyne's and with Roth's own labels in the Hb. of the Bot. Garden of St. Petersburg prove; Roth's description, however, can not but have misled all future authors, as he speaks of scales, no trace of which is present in the different specimens I had occasion to examine, not even in Roth's own, nor are the flowers usually 4-parted, but almost always 5-parted.

Boissier l. c. already mentions that the capsule bursts irregularly; whether it more readily opens when fully ripe, is unknown, but in all the specimens examined it rather adheres to the base in the calyx, and bursts only when some force is used, the deeply bilobed lower part of the dissepiment remaining with the base. It therefore very properly comes in at the end of this section, uniting it with the next.

With *C. Californica* this species is closely connected, and, indeed, is sometimes difficult to distinguish from it; but the texture of all the parts is thinner, semitransparent and shining, at least when dry, hence Roth's name is quite appropriate; the adnate parts of the filaments are distinct, but no trace of scales is visible; the ovary is conic; the styles are still more hair-like and on the capsule divaricate; the seeds usually ripen all four, they are triangular, flattened, with the short, almost oblong hilum perpendicular or transverse, both forms being found in seeds from the same capsule.

Sec. 6. *Clistogrammica.*

Styles of unequal length, cylindric, rarely almost absent; stigmata capitate. Capsule never opening at base, baccate, persistent with the calyx, or separating from it entire; intrastylar aperture often large but generally not penetrating into the capsule. Seeds four in each capsule or fewer, sometimes only one; rounded or usually triangular-flattened, often rostrate; hilum linear, short or longer, transverse or oblique, or perpendicular.

Inflorescence variable; either an umbelliform or somewhat globose cluster with pedicelled flowers; or a loose racemiform or paniculate cyme, finally more or less crowded; or (in the 4 last species) compact and often continuous clusters of closely sessile flowers with many sterile bracts. The corolla remains either at base or around the capsule or covers its top.

This section is the richest in species, and the most common in North and South America and on the Islands of the Pacific; one species (*C. obtusiflora*) is a cosmopolite, being found in North and South America, Oceanica, Asia and Europe, and one (*C. appendiculata*) is peculiar to South Africa.

§ 1. Platycarpeæ.

Flowers pedicelled ; sepals united ; ovary and capsule globose-depressed with walls of uniform thickness, (in some forms of the last species conic.)

* Flowers arranged in single or compound subglobose cymes ; styles usually short and thick ; withered corolla remaining at base of capsule.

39. C. OBTUSIFLORA, Humb. Bonpl. Kunth.—Humboldt's plant is the type of a series of forms spread over a great part of the globe. The inconspicuous little species of the Peruvian Andes was not recognized nor sought for in the specimens found in widely distant parts of the globe; these, therefore, received distinct specific appellations, and different ones in different countries. They all are characterized by the bright orange-colored stems (which has suggested several specific names); the loosely globose inflorescence; the obtuse or rounded lobes of the calyx and the corolla, the laciniæ usually equal in length to the tube, and soon reflexed; the thick and at last subulate styles on the large and depressed ovary, which soon after flowering swells considerably, and, leaving the corolla at base, grows into a large, depressed, almost naked 4-seeded capsule, with a large intrastylar aperture of rhombic shape. Seeds 0.6 or 0.7 or even 0.8 line long, oval, oblique, with a long and narrowly linear perpendicular or transverse hilum running almost across the whole umbilicus. All parts of the flower are often, and the capsule commonly, glandulous-dotted. The principal, if not the only difference, I can discover between the different forms, here united, lies in the shape and size of the scales.

Synopsis of the forms of C. obtusiflora.

a. Scales ovate or spatulate.

* Scales small, shorter than the tube of the corolla : Var. *vera*, from South America.

** Scales large, equalling or exceeding the tube of the corolla ; all parts of the flower dotted with glands : Var. *glandulosa*, from the West Indies and the southern parts of the U. States.

  *** Lobes of calyx and corolla broadly oval, or almost orbicular; scales large: Var. *latiloba*, from India.

 b. Scales bifid and often very small.

  * Flowers 5-parted, usually glandulous; scales very small, sometimes almost obliterated: Var. *australis*, from New Holland and China.

  ** Flowers often 4-parted, scarcely glandulous; scales as in the last: Var. *breviflora*, from Southern Europe.

  *** Flowers and scales larger; lobes of calyx and corolla narrower: Var. *Cesatiana*, from Italy and Central Asia.

  **** Calyx large, cupulate, lobes somewhat carinate: Var. *Cordofana*, from Africa.

  Var. *a.* VERA; *C. obtusiflora*, Humb. Bonpl. Kunth.! n. gen. sp. III. 122; *C. inodora*, Willd.! Hb. nro. 3164.—Flowers scarcely more than 1 line long; lobes of calyx very unequal, as in many other forms of the species; scales spatulate, very small and thin, but slightly fimbriate or crenate; capsule 1¼–1½ lines in diameter, dotted with, in the dry state, dark red glands.—Andes of Peru, Humboldt! Guayaquil, Jameson! 542; New Granada, Holton! 544, a specimen with more slender styles; Triana, Linden! 168; Antioquia on the Magdalena River, Jarvis! 1500. This last specimen, with a glandulous corolla and rather larger, more deeply fimbriate scales, forms a transition to the next.

  Var. *β.* GLANDULOSA: Calyx, corolla and capsule dotted with red and shining glands; calyx shorter than tube in some and quite as large as that in other specimens; scales large, often exceeding the tube, deeply fringed, incurved; flower 1–1¼ lines long; capsule 1½–1¾ lines in diameter.—Parasitic on *Polygonum* in most of the specimens examined; Georgia, Boykin! Florida, Rugel! 400; Louisiana, Tainturier! Western Texas, Wright! Bigelow! Schott! Bahama Islands, in Hb. Hooker! Cuba, Pœppig! under the name of *C. Americana.*

  Var. *γ.* ? LATILOBA: flowers larger, 1½ lines long, of a more fleshy, or, when dry, coriaceous substance; calyx and capsule glandulous; lobes of calyx very unequal; these, the lobes of the corolla and the large, deeply fringed scales broadly oval, almost orbicular; styles short, thick.—Martaban, Wallich! Cat. 1320³ under the name of *C. sulcata.*—It seems to differ from *C. obtusiflora* by the more fleshy erect lobes of the corolla, and especially by the more paniculate than globose inflorescence; but it certainly can not be united with *C. sulcata (Chinensis)*, where Wallich and Choisy place it. The specimens are without fruit.

  Var. *δ.* AUSTRALIS; *C. australis*, R. Brown! Prod. I. 491. —Flowers in this as in all the forms, enumerated above, 5-parted, scarcely more than 1 line long, dotted with glands all over; scales bifid or often reduced to one or a few lateral teeth; styles short, usually more slender than in the American forms.—*C. Millettii*, Hook. & Arn.! Bot. Beechy 201, is the same plant, flowers rather less glandulous, styles stouter.—New Holland: Port Jackson, R. Brown! F. Bauer! Caley! Golbourn River, F. Mueller! Canton, China, Millett!—Mr. Mueller's specimen is almost destitute of glands and also of scales; only here and there single or bifid teeth are noticed at the base of the filaments; I can distinguish it from the following form only by its 5-parted flowers.

Var. ε. BREVIFLORA; *C. breviflora*, Visiani! Fl. dalm. II. 231; *C. Tinei*, Insenga! in Tin. pl. rar. sic. p. 14; *C. aurantiaca*, Requien! in sched., Bertol. Fl. it. VII. 623; *C. chrysocoma*, Welw.! in sched. DesM. Et. 71; *C. Regowitschiana*, Traut. Mel. biol. II. $\frac{18}{23}$ Mart. 1855, ex descr.—Flowers 1-1½ lines long, usually 4-parted or 4 and 5-parted in the same specimen, only partially glandulous, or entirely destitute of glands; scales very small, bifid, or commonly consisting of small lateral teeth, or sometimes almost abortive. On the lower Wolga, Liemaschko! 227; Becker! Kiew, Trautvetter; Constantinople, Boissier! Greece, Zuccarini! Berger! Dalmatia, Stalio! Alexander! Naples, Gussone! Capua, abundant in fields of hemp, Bruni! Syracuse, Insenga! Corsica, Requien! Toulon, Quillon! Montferrand, Ramond! Portugal, Welwitsch!—It is often found in gardens on Basilicum, and is probably often propagated and transported with the seeds of that plant; the Basilicum with the parasite is called in the gardens about Naples "Basilico con perrucche," just as the old Botanists used to call the grapes, to which *C. Epithymum* sometimes attaches itself, "Uva barbata."—In France this form has often been named *C. Europæa*, and DesMoulin, Et. p. 67, etc., confounds it with *C. suaveolens*.

Var. ζ. CESATIANA; *C. Polygonorum*, Cesati! in Cat. Sem. Gen. 1849, p. 22 & Linnæa XXIV. 199, not Engelm.; *C. Cesatiana*, Bert.! Fl. it. VII. 623.—Flowers 1½ lines long, 5-parted, without glands; lobes of corolla narrow, longer than the tube; scales usually exceeding the tube, deeply laciniate and more or less bifid.—Piedmont, on *Polygonum*, Cesati! Cashmere, Jacquemont! 876.—The strange fact, that exactly the same form should be found a native of so widely distant localities, furnishes but another instance of the cosmopolitan habits of this species.—Prof. Cesati, l. c., gives the first correct account of the *apparent* intrastylar dehiscence of the capsule in the following words: "capsula ..... ob dissepimenti exsiccationem .. ... hians, ... hinc capsulam apice dehiscentem *mentiens*."

Var. η. CORDOFANA : calyx large, cupulate, longer than the tube of the corolla; its lobes united above the middle, somewhat carinate; scales as in var. *australis;* stamens and style shorter than in any other form of the species.—Fezogl, Cordofan, Figari! in Hb. Mus. Florent.

40. C. CHLOROCARPA, Engelm.! in Gray Man. ed. 1, p. 350 ; ed. 2, p. 337; C. Polygonorum, Engelm.! in Sillim. Journ. 43, p. 342, t. 6, f. 26–29; * DC. Prod. IX. 461, not Cesati.— Along ponds and wet places, mostly on different species of Polygonum, and also on other plants of these localities; St. Louis, Missouri, Drummond! Lindheimer! Engelmann! Illinois, Engelmann! Wisconsin, Lapham! Indian country west of Arkansas, Bigelow! eastward thus far only in Delaware, Tatnall!—Closely allied to the last species, especially to var. breviflora; the principal difference lies in the triangular, acute lobes of calyx and corolla. Flowers usually 4-parted, about one line long; scales small, bilobed or oftener consisting of small lateral teeth; in a specimen from Delaware they are very incomplete, or sometimes almost wanting; large ovary filling the shallow tube of the corolla; capsule comparatively large, thin, membranaceous, of a greenish yellow color, whence the name, which I substituted for my former one, referring to the plants on which it is often found; this color of the capsule distinguishes it already at a distance from other species growing in the same region. Seeds 0.8 line long, oval, compressed, scarcely angled; transverse hilum rather shorter than in the last species.

41. C. ARVENSIS, Beyrich! in sched.; Engelm.! in Gray Man. ed. 2, p. 336.—The different varieties of this species are characterized by smaller flowers (often less than 1 line long) in more compound clusters, which approach in their form to those of the next species; lobes of calyx very obtuse; lobes of corolla almost always longer than the tube, acute or usually accuminate, reflexed and with the point inflexed; anthers broadly oval or rounded; scales large, deeply laciniate-fimbriate, often exceeding the tube; styles rather slender, as long as ovary, or longer; seeds 0.5–0.7 line long, oval or rounded, compressed, with a rather short, linear, often oblique hilum. The differences in the shape, size and texture of the calyx constitute the following varieties.

Var. a. PENTAGONA; C. pentagona, Engelm.! in Sill. Jour. 43, p. 340, t. 6, f. 22-24; DC. Prod. IX. 461; C. arvensis, Beyrich! in Hb.; C. globularis, Nutt.! in Hb.—Calyx thin and shining; lobes orbicular, as long or longer than the shallow tube of the corolla, forming, where they join, 5 projecting angles.—Dry barren soil or old fields on different Compositæ

---

* The article on American Cuscutæ, which originally appeared in Silliman's Journal, was reprinted in Hooker's London Journal of Botany, II. 184 t. 3, 1843, and in Schultz's Archives de Flore, 1855, p. 65.

or other plants, sometimes also on shrubs; from Virginia,
Rugel! Sullivant & Gray! to the Carolinas, Schweinitz!
Bosc! Beyrich! Curtis! Ravenel! and to Florida, Rugel! nro.
400, a. & b.

The western form, with shorter lobes of the less distinctly
angled calyx was formerly distinguished by me as var. *mi-
crocalyx.*—In open woods, on dry soil, on *Solidago*, *Aster*,
Ceanothus, etc., Illinois, Geyer! Missouri, Trécul! Riehl!
Nebraska, Hayden! Indian country west of Arkansas, Bigelow! The latter has often as large a calyx as the eastern
form.

Var. β. VERRUCOSA; *C. verrucosa*, Engelm.! l. c. p. 341, t.
6, f. 25; DC. Prod. IX. 461.—Calyx shorter than the campanulate tube, fleshy and glandular-verrucose.—On dry prairies, often on *Petalostemon*, but also on other prairie plants:
Texas, Drummond! III. 247; Lindheimer! 127; Northern
Mexico, Berlandier! 2457, to San Luis Potosi, the same!
and Parras, Gregg!—Lindheimer's nro. 473 is an intermediate form between this and var. *pentagona*, mixed with a few
specimens of the following.

Var. γ. PUBESCENS: pedicels and all parts of the flower
or only the ovary and the capsule papillose-pubescent.—
Western Texas, Lindheimer! Wright! 1635 (574.)—Wright's
519 and 523 (coll. 1849) are a transition form between this
and the last variety, having the calyx of *verrucosa* and the
ovary and capsule of *pubescens*.

Var. δ. CALYCINA: inflorescence often more compact;
flowers rather larger; hemispherical calyx not angled, lobes
rounded or oval, usually longer than the tube; lobes of corolla broader and shorter than in the other forms, and often
not longer than the tube.—Texas, Lindheimer! 126, (a form
from wet prairies, with smaller flowers); the same! 664;
Wright! both on *Dianthera*, in or along water courses; Martinique, Mad. Richard! 114 in Herb. Mus. Flor.; Herb.
Fauché! (now in Hb. Boissier); Saskatchawan, Drummond!
C. Americana? Hook. Fl. N. A.; Oregon, Geyer! 674.

Specimens from Brazil Eschscholtz! in Hb. Ledebour;
Gardner! 6068 in part, (*C. decora* has also been distributed
under this number) differ somewhat from this variety by
stouter and, in fruit, subulate styles; Gardner's specimens
have also a smaller calyx.

** Flowers arranged in loose compound cymes; styles usually slender,
as long or longer than ovary; withered corolla remaining at base of capsule or enveloping it.

42. C. TRICHOSTYLA, n. sp.: caule filiformi; bracteis ovatis obtusis; floribus breviter pedicellatis in cymulas ramosas
subglobosas congestis; calycis cupulati fere ad basin divisi

lobis ovatis orbiculatisve obtusis basi imbricatis tubum corollæ campanulatum æquantibus seu superantibus; laciniis
ovatis obtusis tubo æquilongis demum patulis reflexisve; antheris ovatis filamenta subulata brevia æquantibus; squamis
late ovatis fimbriatis incurvis; stylis capillaribus ovario depresso multo longioribus e tubo vix exsertis.

Panama, Tweedie! Santarem, Brazil, on *Hyptis*, Spruce!
854, both in Hb. Hooker.—None of the specimens examined
being in fruit, the true position of this species must remain
doubtful. The large imbricate calyx, the slender styles, and
especially the branching inflorescence, distinguish it from *C.
obtusiflora;* the inflorescence the shape of the ovary and of
the styles from *C. Gronovii* and *C. racemosa.*—Flowers 1¾–
2 lines long, "white, with a strong odor of hawthorn,"
Spruce; exterior lobes of the calyx in the Panama specimen
towards the tip verrucose-cristate; in the other smooth, thin
and shining; scales in the former longer than the tube, in the
other broader and shorter.

43. C. GYMNOCARPA, n. sp.: caule filiformi; floribus breviter pedicellatis umbellato-glomeratis; calycis lobis ovatis seu
orbiculatis obtusissimis nitidis tubum corollæ æquantibus;
laciniis triangulatis acutis erectis seu demum patentibus tubo
æquilongis; antheris ovato-orbiculatis filamentum breve sub-
ulatum æquantibus; squamis tenuissimis late ovatis fimbriatis faucem attingentibus; stylis capillaribus ovarium depressum æquantibus supra capsulam globoso-depressam e corolla
ad basin marcescente longe exsertam divaricatis patentibus
recurvisve; seminibus oblique ovatis tumidis tenuissime sub
lente reticulatis.—*C. Sandwicensis*, var. *Mimosæ*, Hook. fil.
in Lin. Trans. XX. 205.

James Island of the Gallopagos group, in immense abundance on Mimosa bushes, Chs. Darwin! in Hb. Hooker.—
Flowers about 1 line long, of a very thin texture; capsule 1¼–
1½ lines in diameter, with a very small intrastylar aperture;
seeds in the only specimen extant light yellowish brown, 0.6
line long, plump, nearly smooth, with a short, oblong-linear,
usually perpendicular, hilum.—Much closer to *C. arvensis*
than to *C. Sandwichiana;* distinguished from both by the
short, broad and very acute lobes of the corolla, and by the
very slender, at last nearly horizontal, styles; from the latter,
also, by the presence of scales and by the naked capsule.

44. C. SANDWICHIANA, Choisy! Cusc. 184, t. 5, f. 4; DC.
Prod. IX. 458.—Sandwich Islands; apparently the only species growing there; mostly on shrubs; Menzies! Eschscholtz!
Gaudichaud! Matthews! Stewart! Maximowitsch! 57; Remy! 424.—Inflorescence a compound loosely flowered cyme;
flowers pedicelled, 1–1½ lines long, "pallide ochracei" Maxim.,
of thin, membranaceous texture; only in Menzies' specimen

in Hb. Banks I find all the parts of the flower dotted with
glands; lobes of calyx ovate, acutish; lobes of corolla acute and
inflexed at tip or sometimes obtusish, often reflexed, but at last
commonly adpressed to the top of the capsule, which for its
greater part is enveloped by the tube; anthers oval; no trace
of scales; capsule 1¾–2 lines in diameter, with a small, almost
circular, intrastylar aperture; styles stouter than in the last
species, somewhat divaricate on capsule; seeds unusually
large, 0.8–1.0 line long, verrucose-reticulate, triangular-ovate,
somewhat oblique but not rostrate, with a short linear-oblong
perpendicular hilum on the comparatively small regularly
circular umbilicus.

45. C. ACUTA, n. sp.: caulibus subcapillaceis; cymis compositis laxifloris umbellulas mentientibus; pedicellis flore brevioribus bracteis ovatis acutis suffultis; calycis late campanulati membranacei lobis triangulatis acutis seu cuspidatis tubum corollæ campanulatum superantibus; laciniis lanceolatis
acutatis tubo longioribus erectis seu subpatentibus; antheris
oblongo-linearibus filamento subulato fere brevioribus;
squamis ovato-spatulatis longe adnatis faucem attingentibus
versus apicem crispato-fimbriatis; stylis capillaceis ovarium
obovatum seu globosum æquantibus; capsula tenuissima corollæ rudimentis ad basin persistentibus indusiata apice libera
stylis e basi lata subulatis paulo divergentibus coronata;
seminibus 2–4 lenticularibus rugoso-reticulatis.

Chatham Island of the Gallopagos group; mostly on *Leguminosæ*, common on a low annual *Crotalaria*, but also on
trees, such as *Parkinsonia* and *Mimosæ*, hanging down in
massy festoons, Andersson!—Closely allied with both other
Pacific species just described, distinguished from them by the
very acute lobes of calyx and corolla and by the subulate
styles; moreover from *C. Sandwichiana* by the presence of
scales, and from *C. gymnocarpa* by the covered capsule and
the direction of the styles; from *C. acutiloba* of the mountains of the neighboring coast and from *C. umbellata* it differs by the inflorescence, by the baccate capsule, etc.—Flowers 1–1¼ lines long; scales adnate nearly to the apex, crenulate on the sides, fringed only at tip; capsule about 1 line
in diameter; intrastylar aperture large, forming a transverse
slit; seeds only 0.5 line long, dark brown in the specimen
before me; (perhaps not perfectly ripe) and strongly reticulate; hilum short, oblong-linear, perpendicular or oblique.—
The specimens examined by me were all on a low Crotalaria.

*** Flowers arranged in branching paniculate cymes; styles slender,
as long or longer than ovary; withered corolla surrounding the capsule
or covering its top.

46. C. TENUIFLORA, Engelm.! in Gray, Man. ed. 1, p. 350;

ed. 2. p. 336; *C. Cephalanthi*, Engelm.! in Sill. Jour., XLIII. 336, t. 6, f. 1–6.—Wet places, often on *Cephalanthus, Salix, Cornus* and other shrubs, but also on *Vernonia, Aster*, and other herbaceous plants; Missouri and Illinois, Engelmann! Geyer! Upper Missouri country, Hayden! New Mexico, Wright! 1629 (124); Arizona, the same! 1626 (578).—In young plants just beginning to flower the cymose-paniculate inflorescence is very distinct; the terminal flowers of the main branches of the inflorescence opening first, and lateral clusters of smaller and ever smaller buds appearing lower down on the peduncles; a little later the fruits occupy the ends of the branches, while more and more flowers and buds are developed on lateral peduncles and pedicels, till at length the whole becomes one large and intricate, and often quite compact, cluster. Short pedicels gradually swelling into the base of the turbinate calyx; flowers ordinarily 1 line or less in length, mostly 4-parted, later flowers often only 3-parted; tube of the corolla slender, much longer than the calyx, and larger than the short ovate obtuse laciniæ; scales ovate or spatulate, shorter than the tube; capillary styles as long as the depressed ovary; capsule globose, 1–1¼ lines in diameter, bearing the withered corolla on top, often with only 1 or 2 seeds; seeds 0.6–0.7 line long, oval, oblique, carinate on the inside, with a short linear-oblong usually perpendicular hilum.—The western forms collected by Mr. Wight differ from those of the Missouri and Mississippi valleys only by having larger flowers (1.2–1.4 lines long), larger, more depressed, mostly 4-seeded capsules (1½–2 lines in diameter) and larger (0.8 line long) flatter seeds.

Choisy in DC. Prod. IX. 458, wrongly gives this very distinct species as a synonym of *C. compacta*, with which it has scarcely any thing in common but the hooded capsule; from small flowered forms of *C. Gronovii* it differs by the position of the dead corolla and by the structure of the ovary and capsule.

47. C. CALIFORNICA, Choisy! Cusc. 183; DC. Prod. IX., 457; Hook & Arn.! Bot. Beechy, 364.—Both authors described this plant from Douglas' specimens under the same name and in the same year, (1841); Nuttall, in the Hb. Acad. Philad., had named it *C. acuminata*.—Flowers on slender pedicels, loosely paniculate; calyx small, turbinate with acute triangular, lanceolate or acuminate and sometimes recurved lobes; laciniæ very slender, lanceolate-linear, acute or acuminate, erect or spreading, in fruit mostly erect or connivent; scales wanting, or indicated by a membranaceous inverted arch, with a smooth or crenulate margin connecting the adnate parts of the filaments near the base of the corolla; in a doubtful variety the scales are fully developed; styles

capillary; ovary small, usually globose; capsule enveloped by the corolla; seeds often solitary, subglobose, slightly compressed, strongly hooked, 0.5–0.6 line long.

The different specimens examined vary considerably in the shape and length of the calyx, the proportion of the laciniæ to the tube, the length of the filaments, the indication of scales, the length of the styles and even the shape of the ovary.

Var. α. BREVIFLORA: flowers scarcely more than 1 line long, on short pedicels; laciniæ rather longer than tube; anthers, filaments and styles short; seeds several.—Monterey in fields, Hartweg! 1863.

Var. β. GRACILIFLORA: flowers slender, 1½–2½ lines long; calyx often shorter than tube of corolla; laciniæ as long as the tube, very narrow; filaments often short, or as long or longer than the linear-oblong anthers, styles as long or much longer than ovary.—California, Douglas! Fremont! 506; Bigelow!

Var. γ. LONGILOBA: Flowers 2–2½ lines long; calyx usually equal to the tube, rarely shorter, sometimes longer; laciniæ slender, sometimes twice the length of the tube; subulate filaments as long or longer than the oblong-linear anthers; styles very long and slender.—California, principally, as it appears, on the coast of the southern parts of the State and commonly on some species of *Eriogonum*: Sta. Barbara, Nuttall! San Diego, Thurber! 570 & 633; Newberry!

Var. δ. APICULATA: corolla somewhat granulate, ovary and 1-seeded capsule conic, apiculate; otherwise very similar to the last.—On the Colorado, Bigelow! in February.

Var. ε. ? SQUAMIGERA: flowers 2–2½ lines long, on pedicels shorter than the flower, or even the calyx, in rather crowded subglobose clusters; lobes of calyx lanceolate, acuminate, as long as the open, funnel-shaped tube of the corolla; laciniæ lanceolate, as long as the tube, at last spreading; anthers oblong-linear, cordate at base, on very short filaments; scales spatulate, fringed, shorter than the tube, incurved; styles as long as the very acute ovarium; capsule apiculate, 1-seeded, lower half enveloped by the tube of the corolla.—The more densely clustered flowers, the presence of scales and the acute ovarium would seem to specifically distinguish this form, but the last mentioned variety appears to unite it with the common form; perhaps it ought to be classed with the next species.—Saline soil on the Rio Virgen, Utah, on *Suæda*, J. Remy! in Hb. Mus. Paris.

§ 2. Oxycarpeæ.

Flowers subsessile, or pedicelled; sepals united; ovary and capsule thickened towards the apex, usually more or less conic.

4

* Flowers subsessile, crowded in rather dense, small or large and compound glomerules; withered corolla enveloping or covering the 1-2-seeded capsule.

48. C. SUBINCLUSA, Durand & Hilgard! in Jour. Ac. Phil. III. p. 42, and in Pacif. R.R. Rep. V. 3, p. 11.—This fine and large flowered species resembles different forms of *C. corymbosa* and *C. odontolepis* so much, that I felt considerably inclined to unite all of them as varieties of one and the same species; but then the dehiscence or nondehiscence of the capsule would have to be considered as a character of not even specific importance; there are, however, also other differences, so that these species must be viewed as representing different types under a similar external form.—Flowers 2–3 lines long, on very short pedicels or almost sessile, paniculate-glomerate, at last forming large and rather dense clusters; cylindrical tube of corolla longer than the deeply divided calyx; lobes fleshy, ovate lanceolate, acutish, imbricate; laciniæ ovate, acute, more or less crenulate, shorter than the tube, erect or patulous; anthers oblong or ovate, cordate, usually longer than the filaments, or even subsessile; scales scarcely reaching above the middle of the tube, spatulate-oblong, deeply fringed; styles slender, much longer than the 2-pointed ovary, at first scarcely exsert; capsule oval, 1-2-seeded, its upper part capped by the withered corolla; seeds 0.7–0.9 line in diameter, rough, oval or subglobose, oblique or almost hooked, with a very small oblong hilum.

On the Tejon Pass in the southern part of California, on *Salix* and *Artemisia*, Heermann! in the same region on *Cratægus*, Le Conte! Sierra Nevada, above Placerville, Remy! Saline marshes on Mare Island, Bay of San Francisco, on *Grindelia*, Wright!—It is remarkable, but in this genus not unusual, that specimens from the high mountains are absolutely identical with those from the salt marshes of the coast; the only difference I can discover consists in the flower being a little larger, the filaments longer and the anther shorter.

Var. β. ABBREVIATA: lobes of calyx more membranaceous, less deeply divided, scarcely imbricate, rather longer than the short funnel-shaped tube of the corolla; laciniæ as long as tube; styles as long as the conic ovary, shorter than the oval capsule which is entirely enveloped by the corolla.—Mare Island in San Francisco Bay, on *Arthrocnemon*, Wright!

49. C. MICRANTHA, Choisy! Cusc. 175, t. 1, f. 3, DC. Prod. IX., 453; Gay! Fl. Chil. IV. 446.—A small flowered and low species, perhaps the lowest one in South America, peculiar to Chili: Coquimbo, on the shore of the Ocean, always on *Frankenia*, Cl. Gay! 538; Concon, on *Plantago, Trifolium*, etc., Pœppig! 89 under the name of *C. Popayanensis;*

St. Jago, Dr. Philippi! Besser!—Flowers about one line long
on short pedicels or almost sessile, in small compact clusters;
lobes of calyx and corolla broadly triangular, acute, the latter often somewhat crenulate; scales usually small, ovate or
spatulate, attached to the middle of the tube and scarcely
reaching to the throat; styles capillary, usually much shorter
than the conic ovary; stigmas rather small but very distinctly capitate, so that it is difficult to understand how Choisy
could place this species among those with filiform stigmas;
even his own figure, though not quite correct, does not bear
him out.—Capsule oval, 1-seeded, enveloped in the corolla,
with top naked; seed 0.6 line long, compressed obovate, rostrate, rough, with a very small hilum reduced to almost a
point. This is Choisy's original plant, from Coquimbo; all
the other specimens cited above belong to

Var. β. LATIFLORA: flowers rather larger, 1¼-1½ lines long,
petals spreading, scales often larger, styles longer; fruit not
seen. Some of Pœppig's plants approach the original specimens by their small flowers and crenulate laciniæ.

** Flowers pedicelled, disposed in rather loose paniculate cymes, which
often at last become crowded; withered corolla usually enveloping the
capsule or covering its top, in the three last species investing only its base.

† Lobes of corolla acute or rarely obtuse, inflexed or corniculate at the
apex.

50. C. DECORA, Choisy, under the name of *indecora;*
Choisy saw only a very poor blackened specimen, such as
Berlandier was in the habit of making, of the small flowered
variety; but it so happens that this is one of the prettiest
species, so much so, that Scheele has named it *pulcherrima;*
I therefore feel justified in the liberty I take with Choisy's
name in lopping off its negative *in.*—This is a wide spread
and quite variable species, extending from the United States
to Brazil, always readily recognized by the structure of the
fleshy white flowers, which consist of large convex cells,
which make the surface appear rough and the margin crenulate; these cells are on the surface sometimes elongated into
oval or cylindric papillæ; inflorescence loosely paniculate or
in some forms at last more compact; lobes of calyx ovate or
lanceolate, acute, of different lengths; laciniæ ovate-lanceolate, inflexed at the acute point, erect or spreading, not recurved; scales large, broadly oval; styles usually stout and
very unequal; about as long as the conic ovary; capsule enveloped by the corolla; seeds usually several, 0.6–0.9 line
long, obliquely ovate, rostrate, rough, with a very short, oblong, transverse hilum. The following varieties may be distinguished.

Var. α. INDECORA; *C. indecora*, Choisy! Cusc. 182, t. 3, f. 3; DC. Prod. IX. 457; *C. neuropetala*, β. *minor*, Engelm.! in Boston Journ. N. Hist. V. 223; flowers 1–1¼ lines long, on long pedicels, loosely panicled, with very short calyx.—On the Rio Grande, Berlandier! 865 & 2285; Texas, Lindheimer! 123, (in some of the distributed collections the numbers 123 and 124, both forms of this species, are transposed).—A papillose-hispid form of this variety is *C. verrucosa*, α. *hispidula* Englm.! Sill. Jour. 43, p. 341; *C. hispidula*, Engelm.! ib. 45, p. 75; DC. Prod. IX. 461; Texas, Berlandier! 956 & 2386; Drummond! 248; Lindheimer! 474; Wright! Some of these specimens by their larger flowers approach the next form.

Var. β. PULCHERRIMA; *C. neuropetala*, Engelm.! l. c. 45, p. 75; DC. Prod. IX. 461; *C. pulcherrima*, Scheele! in Linnæa 21, p. 750; smooth or rarely slightly papillose; inflorescence loose or sometimes more compact; flowers variable in size, 1¼–1¾ lines long, usually broadly campanulate; calyx as long or longer than tube; styles usually as long as ovary, rarely much longer; anthers and stigmas yellow or often purple. A form with very large and broad flowers is *C. neuropetala*, γ *littoralis*, Engelm. Boston Journ. l. c.—On wet and dry prairies, from the seacoast to the mountains, on different shrubs, also on herbaceous *Compositæ, Leguminosæ*, etc.: south-western Illinois, Engelmann! Indian country west of Arkansas, Fremont! 2d Exp. 485; Bigelow! Texas, Lindheimer! 124 (a very large flowered form) 474, 475; and westward, Wright! coll. 1849, nros. 520, 521, 524, 525; coll. 1851–'52, nros. 1630, 1633, 1634, 1637, 1638; Sonora, Wright! 1622; Northern Mexico, Gregg! 78 and 888; Florida, Chapman! St. Marks, Rugel! 1000 & 1001; Cuba, Hb. Vind.! Jamaica, McFaddin! Bancroft! a small flowered, short styled form; Cumming! 95; Alexander! Brazil, Salzmann! in Hb. Buchinger; Gardner! 5036, a form with very long styles, and 6068 in part (*C. arvensis* var. has been distributed under the same number.)

Var. γ. SUBNUDA: lower half of capsule enveloped by the tough remains of the corolla, upper part naked; short styles divaricate.—"Common on the overflowed islands of the Parana," Brazil, Tweedie! in Hb. Hooker.

Var. δ. INTEGRIUSCULA: calyx shorter than the deeply campanulate tube of the corolla; laciniæ erect; scales triangular, acutish, thin, almost entire; styles capillary, shorter than ovary.—Mendoza, on *Ephedra*, Gillies!

51. C. INFLEXA; *C. Coryli*, Engelm.! in Sill. Journ. 43, p. 337; *C. umbrosa*, Beyrich! in Hb. reg. Berol. in part, not Hooker; Engelm.! in Gray Man. ed. 1, 351; ed. 2, 336; *C. parviflora*, Nutt.! in Hb.; *C. congesta*, Beyr.! in Hb.; *C.*

compacta, var. *crenulata*, Choisy in DC. Prod. IX. 459.—In open woods or dry prairies, usually on shrubs, *Corylus*, *Ceanothus*, *Symphoricarpus*, *Rhus*, *Salix* and even on *Carya*, but also on *Helianthus*, *Solidago* and other Compositæ, etc. Virginia, Beyrich! Gray & Sullivant! Georgia, Beyrich! Illinois and Missouri, Engelmann! Riehl! Kansas, Fendler! 658; region west of Arkansas, Bigelow! on the Upper Missouri and Yellowstone rivers, Hayden!—Flowers 1 line long, of similar structure as the last; distinguished by the deeper, subcylindric, mostly 4-parted corolla, which at last covers only the top of the capsule, the erect, inflexed laciniæ and the minute scales, reduced to lateral teeth; styles of different lengths, divaricate on capsule; seeds ovate, oblique, thick, 0.6–0.7 line long, with a small, oblong, oblique or transverse hilum.

52. C. APPENDICULATA, n. sp.: caulibus capillaceis; cymis fasciculato-paniculatis laxifloris; calycis brevissimi basi glanduloso-appendiculati lobis ovatis acutis tubum profunde campanulatum vel subcylindricum dimidium vix æquantibus; laciniis ovato-lanceolatis demum reflexis apice acuto incurvis tubo æquilongis; antheris ovato-orbiculatis cordatis filamento longioribus; squamis obovatis crispato-fimbriatis faucem æquantibus incurvis; stylis tenuibus ovario acuto subæqualibus; capsula globosa apiculata sub-1-sperma exserta supra medium nuda, foramine intrastylari magno; seminibus ovatosubglobosis obliquis.

Cape of Good Hope, on *Erica* and other shrubs: Zwellendam, "on dry hills throughout the whole district," Kraus! nro. 1816, under the name of *C. Africana;* Teufelsberg, in Hb. Fischer! now Hb. H. B. Petropol.—The only South African species belonging to this section; distinguished by the very small (scarcely ¼ line long) appendiculate calyx, etc.; flowers 1–1¼ lines long; seeds 0.6 line long.

53. C. STENOLEPIS, n. sp.: caulibus capillaceis; cymis paniculatis laxis paucifloris; pedicellis elongatis bractea ovata suffultis; calycis turbinati glandulosi lobis ovatis obtusis tubo corollæ subcylindrico brevioribus; laciniis tubo brevioribus lanceolatis reflexis apice acutiusculo incurvis; staminibus brevissimis, anthera ovata filamento subulato æquilonga; squamis angustissimis parce fimbriatis faucem vix attingentibus incurvis; stylis ovarium conicum bicuspe subæquantibus demum exsertis; capsula globosa apiculata sub-1-sperma apice corolla calyptræformi tecta; seminibus subglobosis asperatis.

Andes of Quito, Fr. Hall! in Hb. reg. Berol.; J. P. Couthouy! on a *Dalea* "on the banks of the Machange, 9,500 feet high."—A very distinct species covering low shrubs with intricate masses of their hair-like stems, with scattered loosely flowered panicles; whole plant filled with a reddish yellow juice; flowers scarcely more than 1 line long; scales very narrow, linear, irregularly and sparsely laciniate-fimbriate towards the tip; seeds 0.7 line long.

54. C. CORNICULATA, n. sp.: caulibus filiformibus crassiusculis; cymis bracteosis laxis paniculatis seu magis compactis subglobosis; bracteis membranaceis ovatis obtusis; floribus pedicellatis; calycis campanulati ultra medium fissi lobis ovatis carinatis basi imbricatis obtusis seu cuspide nodosoincrassato obtusato apiculatis subinde patulis recurvisve corollæ tubum æquantibus seu superantibus; laciniis tubo æquilongis ovato-lanceolatis demum patulis reflexisve apice nodigero seu cucullato corniculatis inflexis; antheris oblongis filamenta subulata æquantibus; squamis late ovatis fimbriato-fissis tubum excedentibus incurvis; stylis ovarium pyriforme æquantibus, stigmatibus magnis pileatis; capsula corolla marcescente inclusiata apice nuda, orificio intrastylari magno; seminibus oblique ovatis intus carinatis.

Var. α. RACEMULOSA: floribus laxe paniculato-cymosis; calycis lobis apice nodoso acutiusculis.—Southern Brazil, Sellow! 2489 and 3621 in Hb. reg. Berol.

Var. β. SPHÆROCYMA: floribus globoso-cymosis; calycis lobis acutiusculis seu obtusis.—Brazil, Prov. Goyaz, on the campos near the Buixas, Weddell! Venezuela, on the Rio Meta, Karsten!

This is the first of a series of intricate, mostly Brazilian species, which includes nros. 54–58, and which will not be entirely cleared up until carefully studied in their native homes. The inflexed-pointed laciniæ and the naked capsule with the large intrastylar orifice seem to distinguish it sufficiently from C. racemosa. Whether both forms described above, which seem to differ so materially in their inflorescence, really do belong together, must be decided after a fuller study of this whole group; Weddell's specimen seems to connect them.—Flowers 1–1¾ lines long; cymes of one 5–8 lines, glomerules of the other 4–5 lines in diameter; seeds of the largest flowered specimen 0.6–0.7 line long, obliquely ovate, with a very short linear-oblong transverse hilum.

55. C. RACEMOSA, Martius; spread in several forms over a great part of South America, just like C. Gronovii over North America, and C. planiflora over Asia and the Mediterranean regions; it has been introduced with agricultural seeds into Europe, where it has given rise to many discussions, and has, to some extent, stimulated botanists to a further examination of this genus.—All the forms of this species are characterized by the loose racemose-paniculate inflorescense; calyx usually shorter than the deeply campanu-

late gradually widening tube; laciniæ commonly short, spreading or reflexed with inflexed points; scales large; ovarium ovate or obovate, the upper part being compact; styles stout with large, depressed, almost peltate stigmas; capsule commonly enveloped by the corolla, with 2–4 light brown, oval, obliquely truncate or rostrate seeds, 0.6–0.7 line in length; hilum short, linear, perpendicular or transverse, often with radiating lines on the umbilicus. I distinguish the following forms:

Var. α. BRASILIANA; *C. racemosa;* Martius! itin. I. 286; Choisy! Cusc. 181, t. 3, f. 1; DC. Prod. IX. 456; flowers with few or scarcely any glands, of a rather membranaceous texture and pale color, with very short and obtuse lobes of calyx and obtusish lobes of corolla; flowers usually 1½ lines long.—Common about Rio and generally in Brazil, on shrubs and herbaceous plants; Martius! 941; Booz! Gaudichaud! Graham! Pohl! 5100, in part; Riedel, 695.

Var. β. MINIATA: *C. miniata*, Martius! l. c.; var. *minuta*, Choisy! l. c.; flowers of a thicker texture, reddish, more or less glandulous.—Brazil, Martius! 1292; Ackermann! Mikan! Langsdorff! Pohl! 5100 in part; Vauthier! 252; Lund! 737.

Var. γ. CHILIANA; *C. Chilensis*, Bertero! in sched., not Ker; *C. suaveolens*, Seringe, Ann. Sc. phys. nat. Lyon, 1840; Cl. Gay! Fl. chil. IV. 448; DesM. Et. 66 (under *Cassutha*, and confounded with *C. obtusiflora*, var. *breviflora*); *C. corymbosa*, Choisy! Cusc. 180; DC. Prod. IX. 456, not Ruiz & Pav.; *C. Hassiaca*, Pfeiffer! Bot. Zeit. 1843, p. 705; *Eng. migrans*, Pf. ib, 1845, p. 674; *C. diaphana*, Wend. Fl. hass. 364; *C. Popayanensis*, Pœppig! in Hb. Vind. not H.B.K.—Flowers larger, 1½–2 lines long, more membranaceous; lobes of corolla with acute inflexed points; scales as long as, or often shorter, than the tube.—Chili, Bertero! 205 in Hb. DC., 940 & 201 in Hb. Shuttleworth (nro. 940 in Hb. DC. is *C. Chilensis*); Pœppig! Cl. Gay! 449; about twenty years ago it was introduced into Europe, but is apparently now lost; on *Medicago sativa*, sometimes, in wet seasons, destroying whole fields; also parasitic on many other plants growing about such fields; it has been observed in France, Piedmont, Switzerland, Germany and Holland.

Var. δ. CALYCINA; *C. suaveolens*, Lechler! in sched.; flowers as large as in the last, often glandulous, with longer and obtusish lobes of calyx and corolla, both as long as the short and wide tube; dead corolla covering the capsule.—Brazil, Sellow! in Hb. reg. Berol., Weddell! Riedel! Valdivia, Lechler! 479.

Var. ε. NUDA; *C. citricola*, Schlecht. Linn. XXII. 808? Lobes of glandular calyx ovate, nearly as long as the tube of the corolla; laciniæ of same length, reflexed, at the obtusish apex inflexed; styles as long as the conic ovary, at last divaricate; lower part of the depressed somewhat glandulous capsule covered by the corolla, upper half free.—Brazil, near Rio, Sellow! 4.99 B.; southern Brazil, the same! in Hb. reg. Berol.; Riedel! 990 in Hb. H. B. Petrop.; Island of Sta. Catarina, southern Brazil, on *Citrus*, Pabst ex Schlechtend.

56. C. PARVIFLORA, n. sp.: caulibus capillaceo-filiformibus intricatis; cymis fasciculato-paniculatis laxis paucifloris; pedicellis flore minuto late campanulato longioribus; calycis turbinati lobis ovatis obtusiusculis tubum corollæ æquantibus; laciniis ovatis seu lanceolatis patulis apice obtusiusculo inflexis; staminibus brevibus, antheris ovatis filamenta æquantibus; squamis ovatis laciniato-fimbriatis conniventibus; stylis ovario obovato æquilongis.—*C. micrantha*, Martius! in Hb., not Choisy.

Var. β. ELONGATA: pedicellis elongatis clavatis; floribus minoribus; laciniis acutis tubo subduplo longioribus demum reflexis; filamentis subulatis gracilibus lacinias æquantibus.

Brazil, Minas Geraes, on *Trembleya*, Ackermann! Villa Rica, on some other shrub; Pohl! 5726; Var. β. Goyaz, Weddell! 2125.—Flowers only ½–¾ line long, smaller than in any other species, with the exception perhaps of the smallest forms of *C. Palæstina*; of a deep red color when dry; limb of corolla spreading but not reflexed; fruit unknown. In var. β. the pedicels are 2 or 3 times as long as the "whitish" flowers; laciniæ and especially filaments much longer and more slender.

†† Lobes of corolla obtuse, not incurved.

57. C. DENSIFLORA, Hooker, fil.! in Fl. N. Zeal. I. 186, not Soyer-Will.—At Port Underwood, on the middle island of New Zealand, on some *Apocynea*, Dr. Lyall!—Perhaps too near *C. racemosa*, but apparently distinguished by the much finer capillaceous stems, the very short cupulate calyx, the short, ovate, obtuse spreading but not reflexed nor inflexed lobes of the corolla, which are only about one-third as long as the deeply campanulate tube, and by the solitary globose seeds of a brown red color, with a short linear transverse hilum on the radiately marked umbilicus.—Flower 1¾–2 lines long, dotted with yellow glands, which Dr. Hooker describes as oil-canals; pistils the same as in *C. racemosa*; dead corolla covering and enveloping the capsule.

58. C. MICROSTYLA, n. sp.: caulibus filiformibus floribusque glandulosis; cymulis laxis paucifloris; calycis lobis triangulato-ovatis obtusis corollæ tubo profunde campanulato bre-

vioribus; laciniis ovatis obtusiusculis tubum æquantibus patulis reflexisve; staminibus brevissimis, antheris ovatis filamenta æquantibus; squamis tenuissimis ovatis laciniatis faucem attingentibus; ovario magno ovato-conico tubum re-
plente, stylis subnullis, stigmatibus capitatis pileatis; capsula
conica apice e corolla exserta.

On the volcano of Antuco, Chili, Reynolds! 95, in Hb.
Hooker.—The only specimen seen is very young with only
few flowers open, and a single half grown capsule.—Nearly
allied with *C. racemosa*, but well distinguished by the large
conic ovary with the thick and rudimentary but nevertheless
quite unequal styles; flower 1¼–1½ lines long, thick and
fleshy, yellow when dry, dotted with darker glands; whole
plant furnishing a deep yellow dye.

59. C. CRISTATA, n. sp.: caulibus filiformibus; floribus
breviter pedicellatis cymoso-paniculatis basi obtusis late cam-
panulatis; calycis cupulati lobis ovato-orbiculatis glandulosis
cristato-carinatis tubum corollæ æquantibus seu superantibus;
laciniis late ovatis obtusis tubo æquilongis, patentibus seu
demum recurvis; staminibus brevioribus, antheris oblongis
filamenta late subulata æquantibus; squamis imæ corollæ adnatis spatulatis laciniato-fimbriatis faucem excedentibus conniventibus; stylis ovario magno ovato apiculato brevioribus
fere inclusis, stigmatibus parvis; capsula depressa glandulosa
corollæ marcescenti insidente supra nuda; seminibus obovatis obliquis sub lente rugulosis.

Plentiful in the province of St. Jago de Tucuman, La
Plata, Tweedie! 1191, in Hb. Hooker.—Flowers on short
and thick pedicels, wide open, about 1¼ lines long; ovary
large, almost filling the tube, subglobose with an abrupt stylopodium in the shape of a fleshy ring; stigma very small,
pale yellowish; capsule with a very small intrastylar aperture; seeds brown red, 0.7 line long, with an oblong, perpendicular or oblique, hilum. Distinguished by the shape of the
flower, the pistils and stigmas from *C. racemosa*, var. *nuda*,
and from *C. Gronovii*, with which it is still more closely allied and which it seems to represent in South America.

— 60. C. GRONOVII, Willd.! rel. R. & Sch. VI. 205; Choisy!
Cusc. 185, t. 4, f. 3; DC. Prod. IX. 459; *C. Americana*, Lin.
sp. 180, and auctt. Fl. am. bor. in part; *C. vulgivaga*, Engelm.! Sill. Journ. l. c. p. 338, t. 6, f. 12–16; *C. umbrosa*,
Beyrich! in sched. in part; Hooker! Fl. bor. am. II. 78;
Torrey! Fl. N.Y.—This, the most common North American species, is characterized by the loosely paniculate, rarely
from the first more compact inflorescence, which at last becomes densely crowded; by the deeply campanulate tube;
the obtuse, flat, spreading but scarcely ever reflexed laciniæ;

the large, oval, deeply fringed scales; the oval, slightly conic ovary. Seeds 0.6–0.9 line long, obliquely oval, rarely rostrate, with an oblong-linear, usually perpendicular hilum.—The following varieties may be distinguished:

Var. *a.* VULGIVAGA, the common form, as described and figured in Sill. Journ. and Chois. Cusc.; it is Willdenow's original *C. Gronovii*, in his Hb. nro. 3160, a very loosely flowered specimen.—On coarse herbs and shrubs, commonly in moist shady places, from Canada and Maine to Florida, westward to Missouri, Arkansas and Texas; I have seen no specimens from the Rocky Mountains or from the Pacific coast. Flowers 1¼–1½ lines long; lobes of calyx usually carinate and like the laciniæ shorter than the very deeply campanulate tube of the corolla; scales mostly shorter than the tube, incurved over the ovary; corolla remaining at base of capsule. Variable in the size of the flowers; a small flowered form is *C. polyantha*, Shuttlew.! in Pl. Rugel from Alabama; sometimes it occurs with 4-parted flowers, var. *tetrameris*, Engelm. l. c.

Var. *β.* LATIFLORA, *C. Saururi*, Engelm.! l. c. p. 336, t. 6, f. 17–21; calyx more membranaceous; laciniæ and stamens of equal length, as long as the shallow tube; scales narrow and longer than the tube; in eastern specimens the flowers are smaller, in western sometimes larger than in var. *a.*—From Massachusetts to North Carolina and westward to Illinois and Missouri.

Var. *γ.* CALYPTRATA; *C. Bonariensis*, H. B. Carlsr. al.; *C. Chilensis*, H. B. Frib. al., not Ker.; similar to the first form, flowers even more deeply campanulate, usually glandulous, rather larger, in very loose panicles; corolla remaining on top of capsule.—Western Louisiana, Gregg! Texas, Lindheimer! cultivated in several botanical gardens in Germany.

Var. *δ.* ? CURTA; *C. umbrosa*, Hook. l. c. in part; flowers small, 1¼ lines long, glandulous; calyx and short broadly oval laciniæ half as long as the deeply campanulate tube; anthers triangular cordate; scales very short, bifid or truncate, appressed to the tube; styles ½ or ¼ as long as the conic ovary; corolla surrounding or covering the upper part of the large oval capsule; intrastylar opening large; seeds few and large, nearly 1 line long, compressed, somewhat rostrate, with a small, oblong, transverse hilum.—Northwestern America, Douglas! Fremont! 79 (1845).—Perhaps a distinct species, taking the place of *C. Gronovii* on the Pacific side of the continent.

61. C. ROSTRATA, Shuttleworth! in sched., Engelm.! in Bost. Journ. n. h., V. 225; *C. oxycarpa*, Engelm! in sched. —In shady woods, on tall coarse herbs, rarely on shrubs,

southern Alleghanies from Maryland and Virginia to South
Carolina, Rugel! Buckley! Gray & Sullivant! Curtis!—
Nearly allied with the last, but flowers larger and wider, 2–3
lines long, scales comparatively small, deeply incised-fringed;
ovary elongated, bottle-shaped; capsule, with the elongated
2-pointed beak, 2½–3 lines long; seeds 1-4, when regularly developed 1–1¼ lines long, obliquely obovate, compressed, carinate on the inside, bluntly rostrate, somewhat reticulate,
with a short oblong linear mostly transverse hilum.

§ 3. Lepidanche.

Flowers pedicelled or, mostly, closely sessile; sepals free, similar to the
surrounding sterile bracts, imbricate; ovary and capsule more or less
conic, thickened and fleshy at the apex; withered corolla covering the
capsule like a hood.—*Lepidanche*, Eng. Sill. Jour. 43, p. 343.

* Flowers pedicelled, loosely paniculate.

62. C. CUSPIDATA, Engelm.! in Bost. Journ. n. h., V.
p. 224; Bot. Zeit. 1846, p. 277.—Parasitic on *Iva, Ambrosia*
and many other herbs, on wet or dry prairies from southern
and western Texas, Lindheimer! 125 and 277, Wright!
Schott! Thurber! to the upper Arkansas, Trécul! Fendler!
N. Mex. 659,b; Marcy! Bigelow! and to the sandhills of
the Platte, Hayden!—A well marked and easily recognized
species; inflorescence loosely paniculate, with many sterile
hyaline bracts on the pedicels and at the base of the calyx;
flowers membranaceous, 1½–2¼ (mostly 2) lines long; upper
bracts and sepals ovate or orbicular, cuspidate or sometimes
obtuse; ovary not globose, as I formerly described it, but
oval, with a thick stylopodium; capsule thick and glandulous at the apex; seeds rarely more than 0.4 line long, obovate, compressed, rostrate, with a very short oval mostly
transverse hilum. The form from Platte river has the smallest flowers, and almost orbicular sepals.

63. C. BRACTEATA, n. sp.: caulibus tenuiter filiformibus;
cymis spiciformibus paniculatis; pedunculis pedicellisque
crassis bracteis pluribus ovatis obtusis, superioribus lanceolatis acutatis stipatis; sepalis similibus longioribus acuminatis
serrulatis tubum corollæ subcylindricum æquantibus; laciniis
lanceolatis acuminatis tubo brevioribus reflexis; staminibus
multo brevioribus, antheris oblongo-ovatis filamento æquilongis; squamis ovatis crispato-laceris medio tubo adnatis
faucem attingentibus; stylis capillaceis ovario minuto multo
longioribus inclusis, stigmatibus ovato-capitatis.

Goyaz, Brazil, parasitic on shrubs, Gardner! 3348 in Hb.
Hooker.—Similar to the last, but flowers much larger, 2½–3
lines long in a rather contracted inflorescence; peduncles re-

markably thick in proportion to the stems; stigmata oval, almost twice as long as they are thick, a form that I have not seen in any other species. The only specimen examined is barely in flower; the ovary is probably shaped as in the last species.

** Flowers closely sessile, crowded in compact and often continuous clusters.

64. C. SQUAMATA, n. sp.: caulibus filiformibus aurantiacis; glomerulis compactis; bracteis 2–5 sub flore singulo arcte sessili late ovatis cuspidatis membranaceis adpressis sensim in sepala exteriora similia et interiora longiora obtusiora tubum cylindraceo-obconicum æquantia transeuntibus; staminibus brevioribus, antheris oblongo-linearibus filamenta subulata æquantibus; squamis ovatis laciniato-fimbriatis medio tubo adnatis faucem excedentibus conniventibus; stylis capillaceis ovario ovato-conico multo longioribus exsertis; capsula ovata apiculata 1–2–sperma corollæ rudimentis calyptrata; seminibus subglobosis lenticularibusve, hilo oblongo abbreviato.

Fields and wastes on the Rio Grande, on *Artemisia Ludoviciana, Helianthus ciliatus* and other weeds, from El Paso, Wright! 518 (coll. 1849) and 1628 (coll. 1852), Bigelow! Thurber! down to Presidio del Norte, Parry!—Clusters 5–6 lines in diameter, consisting of 8–12 flowers; or sometimes small, only 2–3-flowered; occasionally continuous, in the manner of the next species; flowers 2½ lines long, similar in shape to those of the two last species, but closely sessile, in other respects much like the next, but bracts appressed, not squarrose. Seeds 0.6–0.7 line long; subglobose when the capsule has only 1 seed, compressed when it contains 2, oblique but scarcely rostrate, with a very short oblique or transverse hilum, almost a mere dot.

65. C. GLOMERATA, Choisy! Cusc. 184, t. 4, f. 1; DC. Prod. IX. 458; *Lepidanche Compositarum*, Engelm.! Sill. Journ. 43, p. 344, t. 6, f. 30–35; *C. Americana (monstruosa)*, Hook. in Comp. Bot. Mag. I. 173; *C. paradoxa*, Rafin. Ann. nat. 1820, p. 13, & DC. l. c. 461?—Prairie regions of central North America, on *Helianthus, Solidago, Vernonia, Silphium* and other tall *Compositæ;* rarely parasitic on any other plant: from Indiana, Dr. Clapp! to Illinois and Missouri, Drummond! Engelm.! Riehl! 15 & 16; Kansas, Hayden! the upper Arkansas region, Fendler! 657; southward to the Canadian, Bigelow! and to the Liano in western Texas, Lindheimer! Mr. Riehl found it very destructive to the pear seedlings in his nursery.—This, the most striking of all *Cuscutæ,* has been so fully described, that very little is to be

added. The glomerules almost always form two parallel lines on both sides of the stem, wherever it is attached to the stem of the nurse and somewhat flattened, rarely in detached clusters, where the stem is free; these clusters of flowers run completely together and form at last a continuous spiral coil, 6–10 lines in thickness, and several inches in length; the orange-red filiform stems have by this time entirely disappeared.—Flowers $2\frac{1}{2}$–3 lines long, surrounded by numerous squarrose bracts; lobes of corolla obtuse, not acute; stylopodium larger, (Sill. J., l. c. f. 33) or smaller (l. c. f. 34) than ovary proper; flowers often sterile; seeds 2 or mostly 1 in each capsule, 0.5 line long, oval, more or less compressed, very slightly rostrate, small oval hilum transverse.

Rafinesque was no doubt the first to distinguish this species, and his name, a very appropriate one, would have the precedence over the later ones, if he, by his very incorrect description, had not enveloped the whole in so much obscurity, that Choisy's later name is to be preferred.

66. C. COMPACTA, Jussieu! in Hb.; Choisy! Cusc. 185, t. 4, f. 2; DC. Prod. IX. 458; Engelm.! Bost. Journ. N. Hist., V. 225; *C. remotiflora* and *C. Fruticum*, Bertol. Misc. bot. X. 29; *C. Americana*, auct. var.; *C. imbricata*, Nutt.! in Hb.; *C. coronata*, Beyr.! in Hb.—From the banks of the St. Lawrence in the State of New York southward, and on the Alleghany mountains from Pennsylvania to Georgia and Alabama, almost entirely on shrubs, such as *Corylus, Alnus, Andromeda*, etc.; only accidentally on herbaceous plants.— Clusters in fruit often $\frac{3}{4}$–$1\frac{1}{2}$ inches in diameter, continuous and thickest where the stem is twined around the nurse, but also abundant where it is free; tube of corolla slender, laciniæ oblong; dead corolla raised on top of the acutish capsule, giving it a pointed appearance; seeds 1–2, rarely 3–4 in each capsule, 0.8–1.0 line long, oval oblique, lenticular or carinate inside, scarcely rostrate; hilum small, oblong, perpendicular or transverse.

Var. β. ADPRESSA; *Lepidanche adpressa*, Engelm.! in Sill. Journ. 45, p. 77; *C. acaulis*, Raf. Ann. Nat. 1820, p. 13?—Shady woods in rich bottom-lands along streams in the Mississippi valley, on *Cephalanthus, Cornus, Salix, Bignonia, Vitis, Rhus Toxicodendron, Smilax* and some herbaceous plants; western Virginia to Illinois and Missouri, and southward to western Louisiana and Texas.—Tube of corolla wider, more deeply immersed in the calyx, lobes broader, capsule thicker, not so much pointed and corolla not so much raised above it, so that the clusters, especially in fruit, appear more obtuse; seeds of same size as in *a.*, usually 2–4 in a capsule, compressed, scarcely carinate, with a longer, transverse hilum. The difference in the seeds appears to be constant, and proves again that in this genus not much reliance can be put on characters derived from them.

Sec. 7. *Lobostigma.*

Styles of nearly equal length, clavate towards the flattened stigmatose top, which is divided into several unequal orbicular lobes and depressed in the centre; capsule baccate.

Inflorescence a loose fasciculate cyme, bracts at the base of the long pedicels; corolla enveloping and covering the capsule.

The only species of this section is a native of Tasmania.

67. C. TASMANICA, n. sp.: caulibus capillaceis; cymis laxifloris umbellato-fasciculatis compositis; pedicellis elongatis clavatis in calycem turbinatum profunde fissum abeuntibus; floribus glandulosis; lobis calycis oblongis obtusis tubum æquantibus; laciniis oblongis obtusis patulis seu demum reflexis tubo longioribus; staminibus brevioribus conniventibus, antheris oblongo-linearibus filamento crasso longioribus; squamis augustis apice fimbriato bifidis faucem æquantibus; stylis ovario subgloboso fere longioribus exertis. —C. *australis*, Hook. fil! Fl. Tasm. 278, not R. Br.

Hobartstown, Tasmania, Gunn! 1991, in Hb. Hooker.— Well characterized and distinguished from any other species by the shape of the stigma. Fascicles of 4–8 flowers aggregated in larger cymes; flowers 1½–1¾ lines long, usually 5-parted; anthers turned inward, with a very broad commissure on the back; scales crenulate on the sides, deeply fringed and usually bilobed at the tip; styles nearly as long as lobes of corolla, much longer than the stamens, stigma commonly with 4 unequal lobes; styles in fruit subulate from a broad divaricate base, distant from another, with a small aperture between them; no ripe seeds seen.

Sec. 8. *Monogynella.*

Styles united entirely or for the greater part of their length, thick and compressed; stigmata capitate, subglobose or ovate, distinct or more or less coalescent. Capsule regularly circumscissile, usually 2-seeded; dissepiment of the shape of the capsule, transparent, with a thicker rim, entire, no part adhering to the base of the style. Seeds compressed, oblique, more or less rostrate, with a long linear transverse hilum. Anthers sessile, or on very short filaments, often attached to the tube below the throat.

Stems thick; flowers comparatively small, always 5-parted, sessile or on short pedicels, supported by bracts, in small cymules, which form a compound spike or raceme; withered corolla remaining, hoodlike, on the very top of the large capsule.

Parasitic mostly on ligneous plants. Of the 8 species of this section, 5 belong to the continent of Asia, 2 of which extend into Europe; 1 is peculiar to the island of Timor, 1 to South Africa, and 1 to Texas.

68. C. EXALTATA, n. sp.: caule funiculari; floribus breviter pedicellatis seu sessilibus spicato-paniculatis; calycis globosi lobis fere disjunctis orbiculatis concavis imbricatis medio verrucosis corollæ tubum cylindricum æquantibus; laciniis orbiculatis imbricatis tubo multo brevioribus erectis seu erecto-patulis; antheris cordato-orbiculatis ad faucem sessilibus; squamis bipartitis dentatis tubo multo brevioribus; stylo apice bifido ovario ovato-globoso æquilongo, stigmatibus subglobosis.

Parasitic on *Diospyros Mexicana, Ulmus crassifolia, Quercus virens, Juglans, Rhus,* etc., 10–20 feet high, in western Texas, on the Guadaloupe and Cibolo, Lindheimer! 472; on the Colorado and Blanco, Wright! on the Leona and at the mouth of the Pecos, Bigelow! on the Rio Grande, Schott!—Stems 1–2 lines in diameter; compound panicles several inches in length; flowers 2 lines long, small tube hidden in the large calyx; anthers closely sessile; scales reduced to two dentate wings on the sides of the very distinct attached filaments, united at base; upper fourth of the thick style divided; stigmas depressed, thicker than the ends of the style; capsule 3½–5 lines long; seeds 1½–1¾ lines long, somewhat triangular, very slightly rostrate. The large embryo is coiled up in 2–3 rounds; on the upper (thinner) end 3–4 alternate scales may be distinguished. This is the only species of this section, where the styles are not completely united. I formerly distributed it under the the name of *C. gamostyla.*

69. C. CASSYTOIDES, Nees ab Esenb.! in Linnæa, XX., p. 196, sine descr.: caule funiculari; floribus subsessilibus cymoso-spicatis; calycis globosi lobis orbiculatis concavis imbricatis verrucosis corollæ tubum latum breviter cylindricum includentibus; laciniis ovatis obtusis vix basi imbricatis erectis tubum æquantibus; antheris cordato-ovatis ad faucem sessilibus; squamis tenuissimis apice truncato pauci-dentatis tubo brevioribus; stylo ovario ovato-conico æquilongis, stigmate capitato bilobo; capsula ovata; seminibus ovato-triangulatis tenuiter verruculosis.

Cape of Good Hope; primitive forests of Uitehage, Drege, 8037; Hangklipp, Mund & Maire; Zeyher II. 3631 (120.5).— Flowers in spiked cymules, 1¾ lines long, shorter than in the last species; scales united at base, ovate obtuse or truncate, scarcely dentate; styles united entirely; stigma divided almost to the base, lobes subglobose; capsule 3–4 lines long, subglobose; seeds of the size and shape as in the last species.

70. C. TIMORENSIS, Decaisne! Mss.: caule funiculari; floribus racemoso-spicatis seu axi indeterminata apice bracteata spicatis; pedicellis inferioribus longioribus bracteatis, superioribus brevissimis nudis, omnibus bractea ovato-orbiculata concava suffultis; calycis profunde partiti lobis orbiculatis concavis imbricatis tubum corollæ brevem campanulatum æquantibus; laciniis ovatis obtusis tubo brevioribus erectis seu sæpe patulis reflexisve; antheris cordato-ovatis tubo infra faucem adnatis; squamis ad cristulas binas convergentes reductis seu subnullis; stylo cum stigmatibus ovatis compressis ovarium subglobosum æquante; capsula ovata conica sub-2-sperma; seminibus orbiculato-triangulatis compressis.— *C. reflexa*, Dne.! in Hb. Timor. descr. p. 66, not Roxb.

Island of Timor, Leschenault! in Hb. Mus. Par.—The tendency to a regularly spiked inflorescence, which is observed in this whole group, is more decidedly developed in this species; the main axis of the inflorescence is terminated by an imbricately bracted bud, never by a flower; the lower lateral flowers open first, and the upper ones in succession; all, or only the lower ones, are supported by pedicels bearing lateral flowers; the upper ones often have shorter pedicels with 2 or 3 sterile bracts; the uppermost ones are commonly quite short and bractless. Flowers $1\frac{1}{2}$–$1\frac{3}{4}$ lines long; anthers almost sessile a little below the throat; scales very indistinct, consisting mostly of 2 slight ridges converging towards the base of each anther; stigmas of the length of the style and scarcely thicker, oval and compressed; capsule about 3 lines long; seeds $1\frac{1}{4}$ lines in diameter.

71. C. MONOGYNA, Vahl. Symb. II., 32; DC. Prod. IX. 450, & auctt. in part; *C. orientalis*, Tournef.! Cor. 45; Sibth.! in Hb. Jacq.; *C. astyla*, Engelm.! Bot. Zeit., 1846, IV. 276; *Monogynella Vahliana*, DesM.! Et. 65; *C. scandens*, Brot. Lusit. I. 208 ??—On shrubs and trees, as *Salix, Tamarix, Pistacia, Vitis,* etc.; also on herbaceous plants, *Euphorbia*, etc.; from southern Europe through middle Asia south-eastward: Portugal (? Brot.); southern France, almost always on the grape vine (introduced?), Delisle! Requien! etc.; Rumelia, Frivaldski! specimens often mixed with C. *Europæa;* Crimea, Trautvetter; Greece, Heldreich! Orphanides! Asia Minor, Sibthorp! Wiedemann! Syria, Tournefort! in Hb. Banks, Labillardiere! Blanche! Caucasus and Georgia, Hohenacker! Prescott! Wilhelms! Frick! Koch! Soongaria Schrenk! Persia, Buhse! Noë! Kotschy! 713,

Affghanistan, Griffith! 682 & 684.—Vahl's description,
"dentibus corollæ lanceolatis," etc., does not exactly agree
with our plant, nor is Sibthorp's figure, Fl. græc. t. 257,
very correct; but the locality of the former and an authentic specimen of the latter (in Hb. Jacq.) leave no doubt
that both had the plant in view which I formerly distinguished as *C. astyla.*—The inflorescence is a compound spike
consisting of a terminal and several lateral cymes of 2–3
or 4 sessile flowers; the lowest cymes open first and are
sometimes branched. Flowers 1¼–1½ lines long; corolla
1–1½ line in length; laciniæ oval or orbicular, very obtuse,
delicately crenulate, erect, scarcely more than half as long
as the tube, which is entirely enclosed in the calyx; anthers ovate or triangular-ovate, cordate at base, almost sessile a little below the throat; scales attached to the middle of the tube, of the shape of a horseshoe, forming a
narrow denticulate or slightly fimbriate border, which is
sometimes truncate or even bifid; style very short, equal in
length to the subglobose 2-lobed stigma, much shorter than
the oval or globose ovary; capsule 2–3 lines long, usually
oval and obtuse; seeds rarely more than 2, ovate, strongly
rostrate, slightly rough.—*Mon. Blancheana,* DesM.! in lit. is
a form with a somewhat elongated conic capsule, which occurs in Syria and Georgia, and which approaches the next
species.

72. C. LEHMANNIANA, Bunge! in Lehm. rel. in Mem.
sav. ét. VII. 396.—Bokhara, on the banks of the Jan-Darja,
A. Lehmann!—Flowers pedicelled in a thyrsoid inflorescence, slender, 2¼–2¾ lines long; corolla 2–2¼ lines in length;
laciniæ oval, crenulate, shorter than the tube, erect or spreading; scales horseshoe-shaped, attached to the middle of the
tube and covering the base of the ovate-cordate anthers,
which are sessile below the throat; style much shorter than
the oval or subglobose ovary, of the length of the distinctly
2-parted oval stigma; capsule oval. The shape and proportion of the corolla is similar to that of the next species, especially of its Asiatic form; the pistil is like that of the last
species; the position of scales is quite peculiar. I class with
this a form from Asia Minor:

Var. β. ESQUAMATA: pedicels as long as, or often longer,
than the calyx; oblong lobes of the corolla still more distinctly crenate, not much shorter than the tube, spreading,
on the fruit erect or twisted; anthers still shorter; scales almost entirely adnate, commonly showing only a denticulate
crest on both sides; stigma globose or oval, almost sessile.—
On *Pistacia Terebinthus,* on mount Sipyle, near Magnesia,
Balansa! 411.—Flowers 2½ lines, corolla 2 lines long, more
deeply divided than in the allied species.

5

73. C. LUPULIFORMIS, Krocker! Siles. I. p. 261, t. 36; *C. monogyna*, auctt. Fl. germ. al.—On willows, etc., on the banks of streams from eastern and north-eastern Germany, Silesia, where it seems to be common on the Oder, Lessing! Gœppert! Günther! al., Bohemia and Austria, Kovats! to Hungary, Gerenday! and to central Russia, Kasan, Graff!—Flowers subsessile or on at last slightly elongated pedicels; cymes forming elongated spikes, or sometimes more or less compound racemes, which are always terminated by a 2 or 3-flowered cyme; flowers 2–2½ lines long; lobes of calyx oval, obtuse or almost pointed, half as long as tube of corolla; laciniæ oblong obtuse, erect, half as long as tube; anthers oblong-linear, sessile below the throat; scales short, attached to the lower part of the tube, bifid or reduced to lateral crenulate wings; ovary oval, conic, attenuated into the slender style, which is much longer than the globose or oval deeply bilobed stigma. Capsule conic, 3–4 lines long; seeds triangular oval, rostrate, 1¼–1½ lines long.

Var. *β.* ASIATICA: flowers often longer and more slender, on longer pedicels; laciniæ more crenulate and somewhat spreading; anthers on short but distinct filaments; scales entire, broadly oval, fimbriate and somewhat incurved. *C. flava*, Siev. ap. Pall. probably belongs here.—On *Tamarix*, *Salix*, etc., from the banks of the Wolga, Fischer! Becker! where it seems to join the western form, eastward through the southern parts of Asiatic Russia, Caucasus, Hb. Hooker! Soongaria, Schrenk! 229 & 306, b. (the last a form with very slender flowers and longish pedicels); Buchtarminsk, Karelin & Kiriloff! 926; Altai, Ledebour! Bunge! Gebler! 180, to the river Angara, Turczaninoff!

C. lupuliformis, having been published as early as 1787, has by 4 years the priority over Vahl's name, *C. monogyna*, published in 1791, and must stand for the species with all those botanists who consider both plants as identical; but it so happens that *C. lupuliformis* properly designates the species which in Europe and Asia extends north of the 43d or 44th degree, and *C. monogyna* that which grows south of that latitude.

74. C. GIGANTEA, Griffith, notul. I. 243.—On *Tamarix* Siah-sung ravine, Affghanistan, 10,300 feet high, Griffith! 1031 (683).—Griffith's specimens corresponding best with his description are all parasitic on *Tamarix* and not on *Salix* or *Populus*, as he says in his Notulæ, nor are the stems very thick, but rather filiform; otherwise his detailed description, especially that of the corolla, the scales and the stigmas, agrees so well with his specimen in question, that I can not doubt about his having it in view; but he may have con-

founded it with *C. monogyna*, which he has collected on willows.

The inflorescence forms racemose spikes after the manner of this section, but shorter, only ½--¾ inch long, flowers 2½--2¾ lines long, membranaceous, on short pedicels; calyx covering one half of the tube; laciniæ linear-oblong, obtuse, crenulate, a little shorter than the tube, spreading, or reflexed; ovate-cordate anthers very large, subsessile a little below the throat; scales oval, fimbriate, reaching from the base to the middle of the tube; style as long as the conic ovary and the oblong, elongated, somewhat ligulate (linguiformia, Griff.) stigmas.

75. C. JAPONICA, Choisy! Pl. Zoll., 1854, p. 130 & Pl. Jav. 1858, p. 30.—This species extends in several forms along the whole coast of China and to Japan; all the different varieties are characterized by a very short cupulate calyx, with rounded, mostly cristate lobes, which cover scarcely more than ¼ of the corolla; by the oval or rounded, very slightly crenulate, sometimes cuspidate, spreading or reflexed laciniæ, which have ½ or ⅓ the length of the cylindrical or slightly widening tube; by the oval anthers, sessile or subsessile at the throat; by the entire, ovate, fimbriate, incurved scales; by the elongated style, with 2 ovate, more or less conic or subulate, stigmas. Flowers 2½--3 lines long.

Var. *a.* THYRSOIDEA: flowers subsessile with several bracts at base, in a compact, thyrsoid raceme, often 2 inches long and ½ inch thick; scales from the lower part of the tube, reaching almost to the base of the anthers; styles longer than the conic ovary; stigmas short and conic.—This is Choisy's original *C. Japonica*, and also *C. reflexa*, var. *densiflora*, Bentham! in Hb.—Japan, Zollinger! 355; Hongkong, Abbé Furet! Maj. Champion! 457.—*C. systyla*, Maximowitsch! Primit. Fl. Amur. ined., from the lower Amur, is exactly the same plant, with shorter scales, and rather oval than conic stigmas. From *C. lupuliformis*, var. *Asiatica*, to which it closely approaches, it is distinguished by the short calyx and the shape and insertion of the stamens.

Var. *β.* PANICULATA: flowers on short pedicels, scarcely bracted at base, in a loosely flowered panicle, 1–2 inches long and of the same diameter; narrow scales reaching from the base to the middle of the tube; stigmas conic-subulate, as long as style and as ovary.—*C. colorans*, Maxim.! l. c.— Pekin, Kirilow! in Hb. Fischer, now Hb. H. B. Petrop.

Var. *γ.* ? FISSISTYLA: inflorescence same as last; scales from the middle of the tube, not reaching the base of the anthers, broad and often partly confluent; styles united only at their lower third; stigmas conic.—Hongkong, Chas. Wright! U. S. North Pacif. Expl. Exp., nro. 486.

The subulate or conic stigmas, and the often more paniculate than spiked inflorescence, indicate a close approach to
the next species, which to Mr. Bentham was so evident, that
he considered our plant a mere variety of it; but the structure of the capsule, with the corolla persisting on its top and
the dissepiment in its base, shows that it truly belongs to
Monogynella. The dissepiment is membranaceous, with a
thicker centre, but without the thick frame-like border of the
allied species.

Sec. 9. *Callianche*.

Stigmata distinct, elongated, conic or subulate, sessile or
almost sessile. Capsule regularly circumscissile, usually 4-
seeded, dissepiment extremely thin, partly evanescent, stylar
portion small. Seeds compressed, rostrate, angled on the inside, with a long, linear, transverse hilum.

Flowers large, 5-parted, usually on bracted pedicels in compound loosely paniculate cymules; corolla deciduous after
flowering.

The only species inhabits East-India and the adjoining
islands.

76. C. REFLEXA, Roxb. Corom. 104; Fl. ind. I. 446.—
This beautiful species bears the largest flowers of any, in different varieties from 3-5 lines long; calyx with oval or mostly rounded, very often cristate or verrucose lobes, much
shorter than the cylindric tube of the corolla; laciniæ spreading or reflexed, on the margin revolute, much shorter than
the tube; anthers oval to oblong-linear, sessile or subsessile;
scales in the base of the tube, about $\frac{1}{2}$ or $\frac{1}{3}$ its length, with
short and delicate curly fringes, curved; ovary oval, acutish,
often attenuated into a short, slightly bifid style, or with sessile stigmas; capsule subglobose, about 4 lines in diameter;
at maturity, only the lowest part of the thin dissepiment remains; seeds 1$\frac{1}{2}$ lines long.—The following forms are specifically distinguished by most authors; Choisy, however, in
Pl. Zoll. already suspected their identity, and different as they
seem to be at first sight, I can not but consider them as mere
varieties.

Var. *a.* GRANDIFLORA; *C. grandiflora*, Wall.! Cat. nro.
1318, not H.B.K.; *C. macrantha*, Don.! gen. syst. IV.,
305; DC. Prod. IX. 455; *C. megalantha*, Steud. nom.; *C.
elatior*, Choisy! Cusc. 177.—Flowers of the largest size; la-
ciniæ $\frac{1}{3}$ or sometimes only $\frac{1}{4}$ the length of the tube; anthers
elongated, on very short filaments separating from the tube
below the throat; stigmas elongate, subulate, divaricate,
usually on a very short style. This is no doubt Roxburgh's
original *C. reflexa*, as his figure and description, "stigmata

large, spreading, pointed," prove.—In the temperate as well as the tropical parts of India, from the Himalaya, Wallich! 1318 & 1319[2]; Lady Dalhousie! Jacquemont! 1109 & 2183; Strachney & Winterbottom! 1 & 2; Hofmeister! Hooker, f. & Thomson! Sikkim, the same! Khasia, the same! to the low lands of the coast of Coromandel, Roxburgh, and to Ceylon, Gardner! 616; Thomson! and Java, Zollinger! 2839.—The specimens from the islands are remarkably stout, and have a larger calyx than the ordinary form. It often occurs with verrucose bracts, pedicels, and calyx or even verrucose stems; this is *C. verrucosa*, Sweet, Fl. gard. t. 6, not Engelm.; *C. Hookeri*, Sweet, hort. br. p. 290; *C. reflexa*, var. *verrucosa*, Hook.! fl. exot. t. 150.

Var. β. BRACHYSTIGMA; *C. reflexa*, Wallich! Cat. in part, Edgeworth! in Lin. Trans., Choisy, DC. Prod. l. c., and most authors, not Roxb., *C. pentandra*, Heyne! in Hb. H. B. Petrop.—Flowers smaller; laciniæ ½ or ⅓ the length of the tube; anthers shorter, sessile at the throat of the corolla; stigmas short, conic, closely sessile, erect.—Calcutta, Gaudichaud! 129, and valley of the Ganges in general, Jacquemont! 149 & 2520, de Silva! in Wall. Cat. 1319[1], to the Punjab and the western Himalaya, Hooker, f. & Thomson!

Jacquemont, 149, from Bengal, has the corolla and anthers of var. *a*, and the short erect stigmas of var. β; style distinct, almost as long as the stigmai.

C. anguina, Edgeworth! Trans. Lin. Soc. XX., 86, from the Himalaya, is a small flowered form with more deeply divided tube, otherwise the same as var. β.

C. aphylla, Raf. in Spr. n. Ent. I. 145, and DC. Prod. IX. 461, from the Wabash, is perhaps the same as *C. glomerata*.

C. Epibotrys, *Uva barbata* or *Ampelepogon*, is the name given to the numerous capillary stems of a *Cuscuta* which occasionally have been found parasitic on the unripe berries of the grape vine; they often seem to be without flowers; in one instance they have been ascertained to belong to *C. Epithymum*.

C. subuniflora, Koch, in Linnæa XXII. 748, from Asia Minor, I have not seen; it may be a depauperate form of *C. brevistyla*.

C. triflora, E. Mey. in Pl. Drege, from the Cape of Good Hope, is, as well as *C. funiformis*, Willd., a species of *Cassyta*.

ADDENDA.

Page 459, *Cuscutina*, Pfeif. Bot. Zeit. 1846, p. 461, is another synonym of *Grammica*.

Page 467, add to *C. Palæstina*: *C. globularis*, Bert. Fl. it. VII. 625, is the same plant.

Page 478, after *C. odorata*, introduce:

20. b. C. GLOBIFLORA, n. sp.: caulibus filiformibus crassiusculis; glomerulis paucifloris compactis; floribus subsessilibus bractea una alterave orbiculata concava suffultis; calycis fere ad basin fissi lobis orbiculatis imbricatis margine tenuissimo ciliolatis tubum corollæ ventricosum globosum subæquantibus; laciniis ovato-orbiculatis crenulatis imbricatis erectis seu conniventibus tubo brevioribus; antheris ovatis filamento brevissimo longioribus; squamis magnis ovatis breve fimbriatis faucem pene attingentibus; stylis ovario globoso æquilongis.

Cuzco, Bolivia, at an elevation of 11–12,000 feet, Pentland! in. Hb. Hooker.—Glomerules in the single specimen seen 6–7 lines in diameter, consisting of 2–5 flowers; flowers with the thick calyx and the surrounding bracts almost globose, 3–3½ lines long, a little less in diameter; corolla really ventricose or urceolate; ovary globose or even depressed; I could not ascertain whether the styles become subulate; stigmas small and slightly conic; in the dried state, the young capsule seems to be circumscissile even long before maturity; corolla apparently covering the capsule. Evidently closely allied with *C. odorata*, to which in habit and inflorescence it bears a great resemblance.

Page 478, add to *C. Chilensis*:
C. odorata, Choisy! Cusc. 180, t. 2, f. 4; DC. Prod. IX. 456; Gay! Fl. Chil. IV. 447, not Ruiz & Pavon, according to the description and figure of Choisy and the authentic specimens in Hb. DeCandolle, does not essentially differ. The specimens of Gay, 816 & 817 and of Bertero, 940, have a thinner, more membranaceous texture than the ordinary *C. Chilensis*, but Gaudichaud's specimen is absolutely identical with it.

Page 482, *C. graveolens*, H.B.K.! n. gen. sp. III, 122, is the same as *C. Americana*.

Page 493, l. 13, read *Rogovitschiana* for *Regowitschiana*.

INDEX.

The names of the Genera and Sections are in full capitals, of the Species in small capitals, of the Synonyms in common type.

6